The Immigrants' Chronicles

FROM THE SEA ISLANDS TO AMERICA

THE JOURNEY OF

Hannah

WANDA LUTTRELL

D1516206

Chariot Victor Publishing
A Division of Cook Communications

Be sure to read all the books in
The Immigrants' Chronicles

The Journey of Emilie
The Journey of Hannah
The Journey of Pieter and Anna

Chariot Victor Publishing
A division of Cook Communications, Colorado Springs, Colorado 80918
Cook Communications, Paris, Ontario
Kingsway Communications, Eastbourne, England

THE JOURNEY OF HANNAH
© 1999 by Wanda Luttrell

Edited by Kathy Davis
Cover design by PAZ Design Group
Art direction by Andrea Boven
Cover illustration by Cheri Bladholm

First paperback printing, 1999
Printed in the United States of America
03 02 01 00   5 4 3

Library of Congress Cataloging-in-Publication Data

Luttrell, Wanda.
        The journey of Hannah / Wanda Luttrell.
        p. cm. — (The immigrants chronicles)
    "From the Sea Islands to America."
    SUMMARY: Following her kind mistress' death during childbirth,
Hannah is sold to a tavern owner who beats her until she runs away
in search of freedom.
    ISBN 0-7814-3082-8
    I. Title. II. Series.
    PZ7.L97954 Jo 1999
    [Fic} — ddc21

                                                    98-35693
                                                        CIP
                                                        AC

DEDICATION

For the many African-Americans who contributed their skills to the making of the state of Kentucky, and especially for my friend, John Guy, whose artistry in brick and stone adorns many homes across the Bluegrass.

Author's note:
Since the pure Gullah language is practically unreadable by those unfamiliar with it, I have attempted to share only its flavor in *The Journey of Hannah*.

Chapter One

Hannah stood on the wharf, rubbing one bare, brown foot over the other, watching through a haze of late August heat and unshed tears as the small ship that had brought her to Charleston turned slowly and headed back toward the Sea Islands.

She shifted the cloth-covered package containing her other dress and her nightshift from her right hand to her left. She was already desperately homesick for her family and for the soft breezes and sweet smells of Sunrise Island, lost to her now somewhere out there in the Atlantic Ocean off the coast of South Carolina.

One of ten children of the head cook at Riceland Plantation, Hannah was the fifth to be sold. Her oldest brother, Matthew, had been made overseer of the master's rice fields, but Mark and Luke had gone to plantations on the mainland, and her oldest sisters, Ruth and Naomi, had been placed with families in Virginia and Maryland. Esther, a year younger than Hannah, was sickly and unlikely to be sold, and John, Acts, and Romans were still too young to fetch a good price.

Turning away from the sad sight of the departing ship, Hannah saw a tall, well-dressed stranger walking purposefully toward her. Was this her new master, Alexander DuVane, whose wife she had been brought to the mainland of South Carolina to serve?

Master Benson, the owner of Riceland Plantation, to whom she had belonged all of her eleven years, had vowed never to put any of her ma's children on the auction block. Of course, he did not need and could not keep all the slaves born on his plantation, but he had promised to do his best to find good situations for all of those he must sell. Would belonging to the DuVanes be a good situation?

"Trust in the Lord, Hannah," Ma had told her just this morning. "He will be lookin' out for you."

She wasn't sure what that meant. She had always had Ma to look out for her. Now, she was on her own, with just God up there keeping an eye on her. Did He care as much about her as Ma did? Would He be concerned about how she was treated here in Charleston?

Suddenly, Hannah wondered if she would be pleasing to her new owners. She leaned to check her image in the water below, but the waves from the wake of the departing boat broke her image into pieces and washed them away. She straightened and stood as tall as her small frame would allow, as Ma had taught her. She was sure of one thing—the new yellow dress she wore was the prettiest thing she had ever owned. She felt like she was wearing a ray of sunshine, and Ma had even found time to embroider some little blue flowers across the bodice. Then, this morning before they took her to the ship, Ma had tied her dozens of short pigtails with scraps from the yellow dress material.

"I am Alex DuVane, and you must be Hannah," the stranger said with a wide grin that turned his mouth up at the corners and lit his dark eyes. When Hannah nodded in acknowledgment, he went on, "My wife would have come with me to meet you, but the doctor has put her to bed to conserve her strength until the baby comes."

Hannah nodded. Maybe helping care for the expected baby of her new owners would fill some of the aching emptiness in her heart when she remembered little Romans' gaptoothed grin and his chubby little arms reaching out to her. This youngest brother had been laid in her arms just minutes after he was born, and he had been her baby ever since.

She thought she knew how that other Hannah—the one

from the Bible that she was named for—had felt when she had to leave her Samuel. She had heard the Gullah storytellers tell the story many times at the Praise House where they had worshiped on Sunrise Island: how Hannah had left her little boy, just Romy's age, to serve the priest at the temple, and how she went back every year to take him a new little coat.

Hannah was sure their stories would be different from here on, though, for this Hannah wasn't likely to be allowed to go back to the islands to visit her little Romy every year.

"You seem very young," Alex DuVane said, studying her. "You have had experience caring for an infant, have you not? Your papers promised such," he reminded her.

"Oh, yes, sir!" she assured him quickly.

He nodded, then led the way up the street. "Our house isn't far from here," he said.

Hannah skipped a step to catch up. "After my two eldest sisters be sold, I be de eldest girl child in my fambly," she explained breathlessly, not wanting him to think she could not fulfill the duties of caring for the coming infant. "I be having plenty of experience takin' care of babies. Before my pa got killed in de rice fields, my ma had a baby jes' bout every other year! Beggin' your pardon, sir, I don't be aimin' to brag, but I suspect I knows jes 'bout everything dere is to know 'bout babies!"

"Good! Good!" he said, reaching to open a black iron gate and ushering her through onto a brick walk that led through flowerbeds to the front of a tall gray house with blue shutters. He didn't climb the six steps to the blue front door, though, but followed the walk around the side of the house, past a beautiful rose garden with a statue in its midst. She peered closer and saw that it was of a man wearing long robes, holding a bird in one hand.

Her guide rounded the back corner of the house, where vegetables and herbs grew in neat, brick-bordered beds. He stepped onto a back porch, opened a screen door, and motioned for her to go into the house.

Inside, Hannah found herself in a small, dark entry nearly filled with a twisting staircase that disappeared in a turn far above her head. In front of her, a doorway led into a long hallway that ran straight to the front door. To her left, a doorway opened into a broad kitchen, where a short, very black woman stirred something in a kettle hanging over the fire in a huge fireplace that covered almost the entire back wall.

"That's Lettie, our cook," Master DuVane said. "This is Hannah, Lettie," he called. "I'll expect you to take care of her and see that she learns whatever she needs to know. I'm sure she'll be good help for you."

"Hummph!" Lettie muttered, giving Hannah's slight frame a doubtful glance.

"Of course, your first duty will be to Mistress Annabelle and the baby," Master DuVane went on, leading her down the hallway and up the stairs. He stopped before a door about midway down the upstairs hallway, knocked softly, then turned the knob and opened the door. "I've brought Hannah, dear," he said.

A wave of fear swept over Hannah. She had never had a mistress before. Master Benson's wife had died years before Hannah was born, and he had never remarried. What if this new mistress didn't like her? What if she, too, thought she was too little? What if she demanded that Hannah be sold again to some other family? She couldn't go back to Riceland, for Ma had made it clear that Master Benson had determined she was to leave. What if . . .

"Come, little one," Master DuVane encouraged. "Mistress Annabelle can't see you out there in the hallway!"

Hannah edged into the room and stood with her back against the door frame. She caught her breath as she took in the lifelike pink roses that decorated the walls and carpet. Then her gaze fell on a beautiful lady dressed in a white nightgown with lace ruffles at the throat and wrists, propped up by pillows against a tall, dark headboard. Her red-brown hair lay in curls over her shoulders, and her eyes were as blue as the water around the island in the evenings when the sun began to sink into the sea.

"Come over by the bed, Hannah dear, so I can see you," a sweet voice urged.

Hesitantly, Hannah moved closer. The beautiful lady reached out and took her hand in hers. Hannah wondered how that delicate hand could support the heavy gold ring set with an enormous stone that glowed like green fire on her long, slim finger.

"I'm so glad you are here, Hannah!" she exclaimed. "I get so lonely lying here in this bed, with Lettie always busy downstairs and Alex off about his business. You and I are going to be good friends," she assured her, with a gentle squeeze of her hand.

"Yes'um," Hannah murmured, "I reckon I be glad to be here too."

Mistress Annabelle raised her dark eyebrows, then smiled. "We'll have to work on that Gullah accent, won't we, dear? We can't have the baby growing up talking that way."

Hannah stared at her. "Yes'um," she began, then quickly changed it to "Yes, ma'am."

Ma had always insisted that she speak like white folks around the master of Riceland Plantation and his friends. It was only when they were with the other slaves that she was allowed to slip into the soft, slurred mixture of English and the old African languages of the Gullahs. In the excitement and dread of the day, she had forgotten. She would have to be careful not to offend her new owners with her speech.

When the baby came, though, she would sing to him—or her—the lilting songs of the Gullahs, as she had to her own little brothers. She would teach the baby the songs she had learned at the Praise House on Sunrise Island, where the Christian slaves worshiped the Father, Son, and Holy Spirit according to the Bible, mixed with the old rhythms and legends of their African ancestors.

"When will the baby be here, ma'am?" she asked, hoping it would be soon.

Annabelle DuVane laughed, a soft sound of pleasure that told Hannah she, too, could hardly wait for the baby's arrival. Then she patted Hannah's hand. "He's due in November, dear, so we've got lots of time to get acquainted before the great event." Then she turned to her husband. "Alex, show Hannah where the well is, please. I would like a glass of cold water."

Hannah stepped away from the bed, eager to please her new mistress.

"Follow me, little one," Master DuVane said with a smile.

As they left the room, Hannah looked back at the tall bed holding her beautiful mistress, who smiled and gave a small wave of her fingers. Hannah smiled back, then hurried after the master, retracing her earlier steps to the lower floor and outside to the backyard, where a stone well stood in the midst of the brick-edged kitchen garden beds.

"Let me show you how the winch and bucket work . . ." he began, but Hannah interrupted him.

"Oh, sir, I be knowing how to do it! I 'spect I be drawin' near onto a thousand buckets of water from just such a well as dis back on Riceland." *Gullah, again!* she scolded herself.

"A thousand?" he echoed, an amused smile hiding under his dark mustache. He stepped back and waved one hand toward the wooden bucket hanging from the pole that crossed the stone mouth of the well. "Let's see your skill, then," he said.

Hannah stepped up to the winch and began to turn the handle. As the rope unwound, the bucket descended into the well and out of sight. Hannah turned the handle steadily, as her older sisters had taught her years ago. Finally, she heard the echoing plop of the bucket hitting water. She tiptoed to peer into the well, then expertly tipped the bucket onto its side so that it filled with water as it slowly sank. When it was completely submerged, she began to turn the winch in the opposite direction, the muscles in her thin, brown arms knotting as the bucket burst through the surface of the water.

The well was so like the one on Riceland Plantation

that a fresh wave of homesickness suddenly swept over her. How many times had she gone to the well for her ma and lugged the heavy bucket into the kitchen, careful not to let the water slosh out as she set it on the wooden shelf behind the door.

She glanced at the sky. Ma would be cooking supper now. She could almost smell the odors of roasting meat on the spit in the fireplace and sweet potatoes baking in the ashes.

She wondered what little Romy would be doing. Who would watch him? Esther really wasn't strong enough to tote him about as Hannah had. Who would be keeping him out of mischief? Who would see that he did not toddle into the fireplace, or wander out the open door into danger in the fields or woods beyond the kitchen garden?

She could almost see Romy's big dark eyes and crooked grin, looking up at her. "Tell Womie a 'tory, Hunnuh," he would beg. "Tell Womie a 'tory!"

And she would sit down with him on the bench under the grape arbor and begin, "A time and times ago, it was, when ole Br'er Rabbit be traipsin' through de cane forest...."

"Here, let me carry that bucket into the kitchen for you, little one," Master DuVane broke into her thoughts, scattering memories like dried leaves across the sidewalk.

Hannah jerked the handle of the bucket away from his reaching hand. "My ma would have skinned me alive if I be lettin' Master Benson tote my load for me! Not dat he'd offer. But it jes ain't fittin' for the master to be totin' de load of his slaves, Master DuVane."

"Yes, ma'am!" he said with a laugh, drawing his hand back to his side. "I reckon I'm about to forget my place, Hannah! But it's just that you look so small and vulnerable."

"I am much stronger than I appear, Master DuVane," she assured him, careful of her language, lugging the bucket down the brick path and onto the porch steps.

"All right, little one," he agreed. "I will take your word for it. And you may call me 'Master Alex,' and my wife 'Mistress Annabelle.'"

"Yes, sir. I be tryin' to remember that, Master DuVane ... er, Master Alex," she stammered. *Why do I slip back into Gullah when I get flustered?* she wondered.

"Truth to tell, Hannah," he went on, "until we moved to South Carolina and bought Lettie with the house here, I'd never owned slaves. We always had hired servants on our estate in France, but our family did not own people. I'm not sure I like the idea even yet."

Hannah rolled the strange thought around in her mind. She had always been owned, since the day she was born. She had never considered any other life. What would it be like not to belong to anybody but yourself—and God, of course? What would it be like to work for wages and go home at night to your own place?

She was still thinking about it when she took Mistress Annabelle her water, and as she obliged her wish to have her long hair brushed 100 strokes. And she was still thinking about it as she carried the mistress' supper upstairs on a tray and carried the empty dishes back down again.

As she ate the supper of lamb stew and cornbread Lettie had grudgingly set on the kitchen table for her, she wondered what she would do right this very minute if she didn't belong to anybody but herself.

"What would you be doing right now, Lettie, if you be belonging to nobody but your own self?" she ventured, picking up her bowl and cup and carrying them to the pan of soapy water where Lettie had the master's and mistress' supper dishes waiting to be washed.

Lettie gave her a long, hard look that questioned her sanity. "Child, what a notion! You'd best be gettin' them thoughts out o' your head before they get you in a heap o' trouble!"

"Trouble?" Hannah repeated. "But I was just wondering, Lettie!"

"Hummph!" Lettie said, handing her a dishrag. "That'll be 'Miss Lettie' to you, missy!" she said. "And you'd best be washin' up the dishes, girl, 'cause I ain't aimin' to be up all night."

While Hannah finished washing the dishes, Lettie dried and put them away.

"Come along now," she said when they were done. "I'll show you to your room. It's next to mine in the attic. It'll be a little warm from the day yet, but if you open both windows, there'll be a breeze from the sea blow through by and by."

Hannah picked up her bundle of clothing and followed the woman up the back stairs, and up a second flight of steep, narrow stairs to the third floor.

"Go to bed now, missy," Lettie ordered, waving her hand at the narrow cot at one end of the room under the sloping eaves of the roof. "Mornin' comes early around here, and I reckon there'll be much I'll need to teach you."

"Yes'um," Hannah said. Then she added, "Good night, Miss Lettie."

"Hummph!" Lettie answered, shutting the door between them.

Hannah sighed and turned to survey her small room. The ceiling sloped on each side of the room so that her head touched it when she tried to peer out the little window cut into the long side, the one that looked out over the kitchen garden and the well.

She walked over to the taller window in the gable end of the room, and found that it looked out over the rose garden with its statue of the man with the bird in his hand. And if she looked straight out over the rooftops, she could catch a glimpse of the harbor.

The early rising moon cast a silver path across the water, and suddenly Hannah knew exactly what she would do if she belonged to nobody but herself: She would head straight down that silver path across the water to Sunrise Island and the big bed she shared with Esther and little Romy.

Hannah sank down on the cot, hugging her little bundle of clothing to her chest, breathing in the fresh scent of Ma's homemade soap. She fell back onto the bed, letting the tears slide down her face and bury themselves in the lumpy pillow beneath her head.

Chapter Two

"Get up, lazy bones!"

The loud whisper jarred Hannah from a dream of hunting shells on the beach. She opened her eyes and looked up into an unfamiliar broad, black face.

Where's Ma? she wondered sleepily, sitting up and rubbing her eyes. No Esther shared the narrow bed. Little Romy was not sharing her pillow, or curled up in a ball at her feet. She glanced around the room with its sloping ceiling, and memory began to edge back, like the sunlight creeping over the small windowsill across the room.

Lettie motioned crossly for her to get out of bed. "Put you on another dress, girl. It 'pears to me you've slept in that one."

Hannah placed her bare feet on the equally bare wooden floor and stood up. She tried to smooth the wrinkles from her skirt, but it was no use. She had fallen asleep in her new yellow dress, wetting her pillow with tears of homesickness, and never had awakened to put on her nightshift.

"You get on somethin' clean and be downstairs in five minutes, missy!" Lettie commanded. "Mistress Annabelle won't want her toast and tea 'till nigh on to eight o'clock, but Master Alex is likely already stirrin', wantin' meat and eggs and biscuits with jam. Come on with you now, girl! Surely you ain't used to sleepin' 'till the sun's up!"

Hannah shook her head and dug in her bag for her blue dress. Ma had rolled it up tightly, and it wasn't nearly so wrinkled as the yellow one she had slept in, though it could stand a touch from a hot flatiron.

"You can wash up on the back porch," Lettie said. "I ain't

totin' you no pitcher of water up here," she said, indicating the pitcher and bowl on a small table by the door. "You can bring your own up tonight, if you want," she added over her shoulder as she left the room.

As soon as Hannah heard Lettie's feet on the back stairs, she whipped off the yellow dress and slipped the blue one over her head. There was no mirror in the room, so she could not see if her many braids needed redoing. She couldn't do them all by herself, anyway, especially those in the back. *How will I get them fixed here?* she wondered, *with no Ma and no Esther to help?* She couldn't ask her new mistress to help her, and she certainly didn't fancy asking grumpy old Lettie!

She smoothed her hands over her hair. *It will have to do for now,* she thought, as she ran downstairs, her bare feet hardly making a sound on the bare wood.

When she came into the kitchen, Lettie already had a fire going in the huge fireplace and was stirring something in the pot hanging over it. She motioned toward the back door.

"Wash up!" she ordered.

Hannah went out to the back porch. On a small bench beside the door was a bucket of water with a dipper hanging from its rim. Beside it sat an empty basin. Quickly, she dipped water into the basin, splashed it over her face and hands, and looked around for a towel. Seeing none, she dried her face and hands on the hem of her dress and ran back to the kitchen.

Lettie glanced around, dipped something into a wooden bowl, and set it on the table along with a mug of milk.

"Eat," she commanded, "and be quick about it. We must get the master's breakfast on the table before he comes down."

She opened an oven built into the brick wall beside the fireplace, and Hannah could see fluffy biscuits rising in a pan. Her mouth watered. How good they would taste with a smear of fresh-churned butter and a dollop of brown sugar molasses inside them!

Back home, her ma, who had the run of the master's kitchen,

had been envied by the other slaves. All of the house servants generally had it better than those who toiled in the fields in the hot sun, but the cook had special privileges. She could eat and feed her children from the leftovers of what she prepared for the master's table. Sometimes Ma had slipped them tidbits before the main dish was carried by the server into the dining hall!

Hannah sighed and reached for a spoon from the stone jar in the middle of the table. It seemed that here she would be eating grits for breakfast. *Oh, well,* she thought, adding some of the milk from her mug to it, *the grits are hot and not bad tasting.* In seconds, she had scraped the bowl clean.

"Whatever you want me to do, Lettie, jes tell me, and I be doing it," she offered, placing her empty bowl on a long counter that ran the length of the back wall.

Lettie turned to stare at her. "First, you'll be callin' me 'Miss Lettie,'" she reminded her firmly. Then she turned back to taking browned biscuits from the pan and placing them in a bowl covered with a flowered cloth. "And, yes'um, you will do exactly what I tells you!"

"Yes, ma'am!" Hannah answered quickly, trying not to sound sarcastic.

Lettie studied her suspiciously. Then, at the sound of the master's footsteps in the hall upstairs, she thrust the bowl of biscuits into Hannah's hands and turned to spoon grits into a pretty little flowered china bowl. She grabbed a plate of bacon and eggs from the warming shelf above the oven and headed down the hall. Hannah followed her into the dining room, carrying the biscuits.

The dining room at Riceland Plantation is twice the size of this one, she thought, setting the bowl near the plate Lettie had arranged on a small cloth that only covered one end of the table. But this room was prettier, with its rich dark paneling and lacy summer curtains billowing softly in a slight breeze that carried the faint scent of roses through the floor-length windows.

Glancing up, Hannah saw a huge crystal chandelier that swung over the table, suspended from a ceiling decorated

17

with raised white designs edged in gold. A mirror bigger than all the mirrors she had ever seen put together hung over a carved buffet that stretched most of the way down one wall.

On Riceland, things were mostly plain and serviceable. It was not that Master Benson was poor. Rice was one of the biggest money-making crops in the area, bigger even than cotton, and Master Benson was very rich. But here, there was a daintiness that spoke of a woman's touch, and made Hannah wonder if the house had a name to suit.

"You gonna stand there gawkin' all day, girl?" Lettie broke into her thoughts. "Take this urn into the kitchen and fill it with coffee from the pot in the fireplace—and be quick about it!"

The master's steps could be heard descending the front stairs. Hannah grabbed the silver urn by the handle and ran to the kitchen. She poured the steaming coffee into it and hurried back.

"Good morning, little one!" the master greeted her from the armchair in front of Lettie's carefully arranged table setting. "Ah, hot coffee! Just what I need this morning! Later, it will be too hot for anything but cold tea or lemonade."

Hannah dropped a half curtsy. "Mornin', Master DuVane," she replied.

He laughed. "Didn't I tell you to call me 'Master Alex'?" he scolded gently.

Hannah nodded, not knowing what to say, but feeling a kind of warmth spread through her, in spite of her longings to be back on Riceland with her ma and her brothers and sister. Master Benson had not been unkind to his slaves, but unless he wanted something from them, he hardly noticed them.

"I know you must be homesick right now, little one," the master said, as though he had read her thoughts, "but you are going to like it here at Gray Gables, especially after the baby arrives. There will be plenty for you to do then. Meanwhile, Lettie will teach you how to please your mistress." He turned then to his food, and Hannah knew she had been dismissed.

"Gray Gables," she murmured as she left the room. She

knew gables were those little pointy-roofed windows that stuck up all over the roof, and this house had several she had noted yesterday. In fact, the windows in her attic room were gables. And the house was built of that gray cypress wood that made up many of the buildings on Sunrise Island. It didn't rot; it just kept turning grayer as the years passed. She liked the name of the house, she decided, just as she was beginning to like her new position in it.

Of course, that was before she had spent a whole morning literally trotting in Lettie's footsteps! The woman was everywhere—finding dust on the chair rounds Hannah had just dusted, and lint under the beds where she had just run the dust mop. Nothing she had learned on Riceland seemed good enough for the grumpy little woman!

By the time Mistress Annabelle summoned her to her room that afternoon, Hannah was exhausted. She welcomed the easy chore of brushing her mistress' long, dark hair with a silver-backed brush.

"I like my hair brushed at least 100 strokes each day," the mistress reminded her.

"I can count to 100," Hannah informed her proudly, and proceeded to do so aloud. When she reached 100, she added ten strokes for good measure, then turned to replace the brush beside the matching comb and hand mirror on the dresser. Catching her reflection in the mirror over the dresser, she was dismayed to see her dark face surrounded by many disheveled pigtails. She hadn't realized how awful they looked!

"When was the last time those pigtails were fixed, Hannah?" the mistress asked.

"Oh, Mistress Annabelle, I can't fix them by myself," Hannah apologized. "And I don't think Lettie likes me very much, and I ..."

"Lettie likes you as much as she likes anyone, dear," the mistress said absently. "I'm not sure I could make all those little braids, myself," she went on, frowning. Then her frown was replaced with a smile. "You know, Hannah, I think you would look good with short curls. Would you like me to cut your hair?"

Hannah stood in front of the mirror, fingering the mess her once-neat braids had become. "I don't reckon my hair has ever been cut since I was born, Mistress Annabelle!" *What would Ma say? But Ma's not here, and I have to be able to fix my hair by myself,* she reasoned.

"There's a pair of scissors and a cloth to catch the cuttings in my sewing basket by the fireplace," the mistress urged.

Hannah hesitated only a moment, then went to get the scissors and the cloth. She flinched at the first snippings, then sat very still until the mistress had finished and a pile of thick, black curls lay on the cloth.

"Oh, Hannah, you look charming!" Mistress Annabelle exclaimed. "Go look in the mirror!"

Hannah did as she was told and could hardly believe her eyes. She looked so grown-up! Why, she almost looked pretty!

Behind her, she heard Mistress Annabelle sigh. "I am so tired of this room, Hannah! I'd give almost anything to sit in the rose garden beside St. Francis and his birds for just a half hour! But, of course, the doctor says I must not climb those stairs."

Hannah turned her eyes away from the mistress' swollen shape beneath the covers, searching her mind for some way to grant her desire. Suddenly she had an idea.

"Could I bring some of the garden up here to you?" she suggested, trying her best not to mix her languages. "My sister taught me how to cut roses without harming either the blooms or the bush. Esther was sickly, and they gave her easy jobs, like arranging the flowers. She was good at it too," she added, with a fresh pang of loneliness for Esther.

"Why, Hannah, what a lovely thought!" Mistress Annabelle exclaimed. "Alex and Lettie are always so busy, and an extra trip up those stairs just adds to their burden of waiting on such a useless lump as I have become. But the roses will be gone soon, and I'd love to have some here in my room."

"I'll be right back," Hannah promised, heading for the door.

"Put them in that carved silver bowl from the dining room buffet, dear," Mistress Annabelle suggested, "and then come and read to me a while."

Hannah stopped and faced her. "I be sorry, Mistress Annabelle," she said, slipping back into Gullah in her distress. "I can't be readin' to you. I never be learnin' how."

"Oh, how silly of me!" her mistress cried. "Few slaves are taught to read, I suppose. I know Lettie can't."

"Even my ma can't read," Hannah agreed. "And she was one of Master Benson's most valued slaves. But she never forgot what she heard. She named all her children Bible names, from the stories told us at the Gullah Praise House. I be . . . I mean, I was named for the woman who left her little boy, Samuel, to serve the priest. She went back to take him a new little robe every year, you know."

"I remember the story," Mistress Annabelle said. "She had prayed many years for a son and then gave him right back to God when he was two years old." A shadow crossed her face. "I don't think I could do that, Hannah," she said solemnly. "Once my baby gets here, I don't think I could ever give him up. Or her," she added. "Not even to God!"

Hannah nodded, her heart aching with longing for little Romy. But it would be best not to think about Romy. She blinked away the tears that threatened.

"I be right back with the roses, Mistress Annabelle," she promised brightly. "And then I could be tellin' you a story. I suspect I remember every story I ever heard from the Gullah storytellers."

She ran down to the kitchen, where she received Lettie's permission to use a pair of shears and the silver bowl. She filled the bowl with water and hurried to the rose garden.

A slight breeze mingled the sweet perfume of the roses with a tinge of sea air from the harbor a few blocks away. Memories flooded over her—she and Romy hunting shells along the sandy beach, she and Acts and John picking berries on the knoll and then cooling off with a swim in the sea, she and Esther cutting roses for the master's table.

The Gullah storytellers never told me about St. Francis, she thought, as she set the bowl on the bench beside the statue, and began to snip blossoms from the bushes around her. *He must have been kind, though, or the birds would not have perched on him so trustingly.*

When the bowl was full, she stepped back to judge her handiwork. The full-blown pink roses mixed with the delicate pink of just-opening buds made a bouquet as pretty as any Esther might fix, she decided.

"How lovely they are!" Mistress Annabelle exclaimed when Hannah carried the flowers into her room and placed them on the bedside table. "There's just nothing quite like roses, is there?" she asked, leaning over to sniff the sweet scent.

Then she straightened and patted the bed beside her. "Now, come tell me one of those stories you heard from the island storytellers," she said. "Tomorrow we will begin to teach you to read."

"Oh, Mistress Annabelle!" Hannah exclaimed. "Do you really think I could be learnin' to read?"

"Of course, you can, Hannah, and 'we be workin' on your speech, too," her mistress teased. "Now, tell me one of your stories."

Hannah sorted through the stories she remembered, trying to find one that would please her mistress. "Ole ... uh ... old Br'er ... uh ... Brother Rabbit be traipsin' ... uh ... was travelin' through the forest," she began, "and he be meetin' up with ole ... uh ... old ... Br'er ... uh ... Brother Fox ..." She stopped in frustration. "I don't think I can be tellin' the stories in proper English, Mistress Annabelle," she said. "They just ain't the same lessen you tells them in Gullah."

"'Aren't' the same, Hannah," her mistress corrected, "and its 'unless,' not 'lessen.' But tell the story any way you like, dear. We will save the English lessons for another time."

And so the days passed, with Hannah spending more and

more time with the mistress, carrying her cold drinks and flowers, telling her stories, and, in turn, being taught how to speak properly and to decipher the strange-looking squiggles that made up words in the mistress' big black Bible.

Lettie was cross about Hannah spending so much time upstairs, and her tongue was as sharp as her carving knives. Hannah tried to keep her chores done to the cook's exacting expectations, but they both knew that Master Alex had said her first duty was to her mistress. And Mistress Annabelle needed companionship to keep her mind off her confinement.

Almost before she knew it, September and then October had slipped away. The trees outside the window of Mistress Annabelle's room were nearly bare, and the window was kept shut now against the crisp breeze from the sea.

"You are reading quite well, Hannah," her mistress praised one day as she finished her lesson from the Bible. "And your speech is nearly perfect now."

Hannah looked down at the toes of the soft leather shoes the mistress had insisted the shoemaker make for her when he outfitted the rest of the household. Just as she loved the shoes, she loved the mistress' praise, but they both made her a little uncomfortable.

"Now, tell me a story about that wily slave, Big John, outwitting his master," Mistress Annabelle said then. "He's my favorite! And tell it like the Gullahs, Hannah," she added, "for I must admit that Br'er Rabbit and Big John lose their flavor told in proper English, and a 'ghost' or a 'haunt' is nowhere near as scary as a 'hant'!"

When Hannah had finished her story, with the clever Big John again triumphing over his selfish master, Mistress Annabelle clapped her hands and laughed delightedly, just like little Romy used to do when she'd tell him a story about his favorite, Br'er Rabbit.

Hannah was never to forget that cozy November day by the fire in Mistress Annabelle's room, with her laughter ringing out and the excitement dancing in her eyes.

Chapter Three

The first scream jerked Hannah from a sound sleep and out of bed. She pulled on her dress and ran barefooted down the stairs. Just outside the mistress' door, she met the master, his dark eyes wide with fear.

"Get the doctor! Quickly!" he shouted. "It's the baby!"

Hannah turned to obey, her thoughts whirling. The baby wasn't due for a couple of weeks yet. But Ma always said a first baby could come anytime. But the scream! Was Mistress Annabelle all right?

A second terrible scream put wings to Hannah's feet. She flew down the street to the doctor's home, left the message for him to come quickly, and raced back down the street. As she reached for the gate latch, another horrible scream froze her to the spot. Then she was racing around the house and up the stairs, two at a time.

Lettie came out of the mistress' bedroom and thrust an empty basin into Hannah's hands. "Get fresh water in this and bring the teakettle of boiling water from the kitchen!" she ordered. She went back into the bedroom and shut the door.

Hannah went to the well and drew a fresh bucket of water. The ladle shook in her hands as she filled the basin. Those awful screams! She couldn't ever remember Ma carrying on like that when her little brothers were born. But, of course, the gentry were different from slaves. They were more delicately made and their easy lives did not toughen them, Ma said.

Hannah heard knocking at the front door and ran to let in the doctor. Then she ran to the kitchen for the teakettle and basin of water, and followed him upstairs. Lettie met her at the bedroom door, ordered her to get some cloths from the linen cupboard and, again, shut the door in her face. And so it went for what seemed like a long time to Hannah, fetching and carrying, and worrying about her mistress.

Finally, Lettie came out carrying a still, wrapped bundle. Hannah reached to pull the cover back so she could see the baby, but Lettie shook her head and carried it on downstairs, leaving the door ajar behind her.

Hannah peered into the room where the mistress lay as pale as the white pillowcases, looking like a small child asleep in the big bed. Was she dead? She turned to look at Master Alex. He stood beside the bed, tears streaming down his face, one hand holding Mistress Annabelle's. *Oh, please, God, she can't be dead!* Hannah thought desperately. She looked at the master with the question in her eyes.

He motioned for her to leave the room and followed her into the hall. "She's very weak," he whispered. "I haven't had the heart to tell her the baby didn't make it. She wanted it so!" Tears spilled down his face and into the stubble of beard that bristled his cheeks. "It was a little boy, Hannah," he choked. "A perfectly formed little boy. The doctor doesn't know why . . ."

"The baby's dead, sir?" Hannah broke in incredulously. Her ma had birthed ten children, and never had one of them died! Hannah had held the last three soon after their births, squirming and kicking and screwing up their little brown faces in a cry for nourishment. But Mistress Annabelle's baby was dead. How awful!

"Mistress Annabelle?" she asked then. "Is she . . . will she . . . ?"

He shook his head slowly from side to side. "We don't know yet, little one," he answered, and the pain in his dark eyes was so great that Hannah had to look away. "We just don't know," he repeated. He turned and went back into his wife's room and shut the door.

For two days, Mistress Annabelle lay in the big bed. The doctor came and went, shaking his head. She wouldn't eat any of the fine foods people brought when they came to express their condolences and to gaze sadly at what looked like a wax doll lying in a miniature coffin in the parlor. Their faces were long and dark with sympathy, and they were all dressed in black.

In fact, it seemed to Hannah that the house itself wore black, from the huge black wreath of magnolia leaves on the front door to the black cloths that Lettie had draped over all the mirrors. And it was as silent as a tomb, with all the clocks stopped at the hour of death.

"Lettie," the master complained, "I have to have a mirror to see how to shave, and I have to know what time it is or I can't get to the funeral on time!"

"Oh, Master Alex, don't you know the clocks must be stopped in honor of the dead at the very hour of death?" Lettie answered. "And don't you know the image in a mirror reflects the soul, and the spirits of the dead may enter there if mirrors not be covered?"

"That's just superstition, Lettie," the master scolded. "There's not a word of truth in it!"

Lettie wasn't Gullah. She had been born here in Charleston. But Hannah remembered her ma doing the same thing on Riceland Plantation when her pa got killed in the rice fields. She was sure that Master Alex, though, had started at least one clock and uncovered a mirror, for he was dressed and clean-shaven in plenty of time for the service.

Mistress Annabelle came out of her room, dressed in black from her tiny slippers to the comb and veil that covered her hair and her face. She insisted weakly that the master help her downstairs. Afraid to upset her further, Master Alex draped a heavy dark-blue cloak around her and swooped her frail body up in his arms. He carried her down the stairs and placed her in the black carriage that waited by the front door.

"Can we follow the funeral procession to the cemetery, Miss Lettie?" Hannah asked.

Lettie threw her a scornful look. "And just who do you think will be gettin' all that food together for when they gets back here, missy? We've got our work cut out for us to get it all ready, as it is!"

Hannah blinked hard and swallowed the lump in her throat as she placed bowls and platters on the buffet that stretched down the dining room wall. She had been brought here to serve little Alexander DuVane III, and though she never had known him and never would now, she wanted to accompany him to his final resting place under the moss-draped trees of the cemetery.

When the carriages arrived back at the door, the master carried Mistress Annabelle into the house. Hannah heard her weeping softly into his shoulder and his voice murmuring to her comfortingly as he carried her upstairs.

Then she was kept busy carrying the platters of food Lettie arranged in the kitchen, keeping the pitchers of tea and lemonade filled, and washing dishes and glasses so they never ran out as the guests came and went.

Finally, the last guest had gone and the house was silent again. The roses were gone from the garden now, but Hannah cut a small bouquet of pink carnations and arranged them in Mistress Annabelle's favorite silver bowl. She fixed a cup of hot tea and carried them upstairs.

When she knocked softly at the bedroom door and the master told her to come in, Hannah was surprised to see what a small mound the mistress' thin body now made under the covers as she lay on her side with her face buried in the pillows. She carried the tray to the bedside table and set it down where the mistress could see it, but she gave no sign that she knew Hannah or her offerings were there.

"Look, dear," Master Alex said, "Hannah has brought you some of your favorite pink flowers and a nice hot cup of tea."

The mistress didn't respond.

"I will be happy to get you something to eat, Mistress Annabelle," Hannah suggested. "There's all kinds of good things left downstairs. The neighbors have brought more food than we can ever eat before it goes bad."

"You know the doctor said you need to eat to regain your strength, dear," Master Alex encouraged, giving Hannah a grateful smile.

Hannah saw the mistress shake her head slightly. Then she began to sob softly into her pillow. Hannah looked at the master in alarm. "I'm so sorry, Master Alex!" she said. "I wouldn't be makin' the mistress cry for anything in the world!"

The master patted her on the shoulder. "It's all right, little one," he said. "You didn't do anything." He led her toward the door. Out in the hall, he continued, "She's been crying this way for three days now, Hannah. I'm at my wit's end! I just don't know what to say to her! She refuses to be comforted. She wanted this baby so badly. But if she could just get her strength back, maybe we could get through this grieving together and then get on with our lives."

He ran his fingers through his dark hair until it stood on end in places, in a way that Hannah would have found funny in happier times. Now she hardly noticed it, as she searched for words to comfort him. There just didn't seem to be any.

In the days that followed, Hannah continued to bring drinks and special tidbits of food that Lettie prepared, but the mistress wouldn't even look at them. When she would go back to get the glasses and plates, they were always full.

"I just wish the mistress would eat!" she cried to Lettie one evening, as she scraped food from the mistress' plate into the slop bucket, to be fed to the two pigs Lettie kept in a pen out beyond the garden. "She's never going to get strong again if she won't eat!"

Lettie nodded solemnly and went on preparing vegetables to add to a pot of soup stock she had bubbling over the fire.

"Miss Lettie," Hannah said then, "she won't even look at me. She's been so kind to me, and I've grown to love her so much! Why won't she look at me?"

"I think you remind her of the reason they brought you

here, Hannah," Lettie answered, for once using her name instead of the scornful "missy" or "girl." "I think she just don't want to be reminded that you was bought to help with the baby."

Hannah's heart sank. The mistress might never have anything to do with her again! She would always be a reminder of the happy days when they had planned together for the baby. She couldn't help the baby dying. She had wanted him almost as badly as Mistress Annabelle, she guessed. She had hoped he would help her get over missing little Romy. If only the mistress would talk with her about it! Like Master Alex, she felt they could grieve together.

Mistress Annabelle, though, whether she was lying in the big bed crying silent tears or staring sadly out the window at the bare treetops, gave no sign that she knew Hannah was in the room. Lettie had taken over taking food to her, to avoid the reminder of the baby Hannah must bring with her. Still, the mistress refused food, as she refused comfort.

Two weeks after the baby's funeral, they returned to the vault under the moss-hung live oak trees to place Mistress Annabelle beside her baby son.

Again, grief hung like a black cloth over the tall, gray house. Hannah found the air inside heavy and hard to breathe. And, with so much less to do now that the mistress was gone, she often escaped to the garden, or down to the wharf, where she stood looking out over the water, longing for the carefree, sunlit days of the islands.

Now, it was the food from the master's plate that Hannah scraped into the slop bucket. Most of the time, he wasn't even there. He left at dawn and came back very late at night. When he was there, Hannah could hear his restless footsteps in the room beneath her attic quarters, pacing the night away.

"Master Alex won't look at me now, Miss Lettie!" Hannah blurted one day, as she and Lettie were giving a good cleaning to the kitchen cupboards. "I ran right into him in the hall last night when I was going up to bed, and he turned his eyes away and passed me like he didn't see me!"

"You remind him of why he brought you here," Lettie explained. "He'll probably sell you when he comes to himself enough."

Hannah felt fear rise inside her at Lettie's blunt words. Would Master Alex put her on the auction block like the poor creatures from the boats she sometimes saw standing like cattle on the block until they were led away in chains by the highest bidder? Hannah couldn't get the awful image out of her mind.

Christmas came and went without notice in the silent house. Hannah turned twelve, but she said nothing about it.

Then, late one afternoon in the middle of January, the master came home unexpectedly.

"I've found you a position as cook for the Mastersons, Lettie," he said, handing the startled woman a rolled-up paper. "I've put the house in the hands of an agent until it can be sold, and I am leaving Charleston immediately."

Lettie unrolled the paper and frowned at it, holding it upside down in her inability to read.

"Those manumission papers make you a free woman, Lettie," the master explained. "You have served us well, and your mistress would have wanted it so. You may work for the Mastersons or not, as you wish. No one will ever own you again."

Lettie stared at the paper, then looked up at her master. Hannah was amazed to see tears in her eyes. She had always seemed so hard, with little sympathy for anybody or anything.

Master Alex reached out and patted the cook on the shoulder. Then he turned to Hannah. "You, too, have served us well, little one, but I can't set you free," he apologized. "You can't go roaming about the country on your own at the age of eleven."

"I turned twelve a couple of weeks ago, Master Alex," she interrupted.

"Congratulations!" he said, with a thin smile that never reached his sad dark eyes. He cleared his throat. "Anyway, I have sold you to a couple on their way to seek their fortune in the land beyond the mountains. I hope it will be a good situation. It was the best I could arrange on such short notice."

Hannah could not push words past the lump in her throat. Anyway, she had no words to say. She stood looking down at the well-worn kitchen floor until he reached out and raised her chin with one finger, forcing her to look him in the eyes.

"I'm sorry, Hannah," he said. "When I bought you from Benson, I never planned to sell you. But I never planned to bury my wife and baby, either. There's nothing left for you here, little one. There's nothing left here for me, for that matter." Again, the pain in his eyes was so deep, she had to look away.

"Beggin' your pardon, sir," she said, "could you tell me who has bought me?"

Now it was his turn to look away. "Well, you are very small for your age, and I'm in a hurry to leave Charleston. I had little choice of buyers, and I promised Benson never to sell you at auction."

Hannah's heart felt like a lump of cold grits in the pit of her stomach. He was apologizing again. That could only mean her new position wasn't very desirable.

"Please, sir, who is it and where will I be going?" she begged.

"You have been bought by a Mr. and Mrs. Weston, tavern keepers on their way to seek their fortune in Kentucky," he answered, still not meeting her eyes.

"Kentucky, sir?" She had heard of Kentucky, and all that she had heard had led her to believe it was a wild and savage place.

"Be glad your new owners are tavern keepers, little one," Master Alex encouraged, "for they won't be likely to settle in the wilderness, but in some town where they can sell food and drink to the public and rent lodging to travelers. I fear they will be exacting taskmasters, but you don't mind hard work. I don't doubt that you will do fine. Anyway, I've promised to take you to the wharf this evening to meet them. Get your things together, Hannah, for we must leave in an hour."

Hannah's thoughts whirled as she crept up the back stairs

to her attic room. She surely was stumbling through the uncharted wilderness of some nightmare! Surely she would awaken and find it all a dream! But within the hour, she found herself leaving the house, carrying the bundle she had brought with her to Charleston.

Master Alex draped over her shoulders the dark-blue wool cloak Mistress Annabelle had worn to the baby's funeral. "It was my wife's, little one," he said sadly, "but she won't be needing it, and you need something to keep you warm."

Hannah fought back tears, looking toward the harbor where she could see the masts of ships poking into the smooth fabric of a deep-blue sky.

She felt the master take her hand and place something in it. Then he turned and walked quickly away toward an anchored boat.

Hannah looked down to find two gold coins gleaming in her hand. Suddenly, the pent-up grief she had felt at the deaths of the baby and the mistress joined her sorrow at being sold, flowed down her cheeks, and dropped into the dust at her feet.

Through her tears, Hannah saw that Master Alex was talking with a thin, bald-headed man and a tall, heavyset woman. He gestured in her direction, then, without looking at her again, he turned and walked quickly away toward town.

"You, girl!" the man yelled. "Come here! Get these bags loaded on this boat! We ain't got all night before it sails!"

Hannah swallowed tears. *There's no use standing here bawling like a baby,* she scolded. Her life might be turned upside down. She likely never would see Gray Gables or Riceland Plantation and her family again. But there was nothing she could do about it, and as Ma always said, she might as well make the best of it.

Wiping the wetness from her cheeks with the back of her hand, Hannah tucked the coins inside her bundle, and walked toward the boat and her new life.

Chapter Four

Hannah laid Mistress Annabelle's beautiful dark-blue cloak over one of the trunks and set her bundle on it. She picked up both of the bags belonging to her new owners, carried them onto the boat, and ran back for one of the three trunks. She grasped the leather handle and tugged, but the trunk stayed where it was. Try as she would, she could not budge it. It was as though it were nailed down or had grown roots into the stone! She ran to the next trunk and the next, but she couldn't lift any of them.

She looked up to where her new master and mistress stood talking to the boat captain. Master Alex would have helped her get the trunks on board, but obviously the Westons expected her to do it any way she could.

Hannah took hold of one handle of the first trunk and pulled with all her strength. Finally, the trunk began to slide, slowly, an inch at a time. She dragged it to the boarding plank and worked it over the edge. Then she worked it carefully up the plank and over each strip of wood that ensured safe footing. At the plank's top, she let the trunk tip down, but it got away from her and landed with a thump on its end.

"You clumsy wretch!" her new mistress cried. "My dishes are in that trunk! You'd better hope none of them is broken!"

Her new master took in the situation, then motioned for a big black man who was effortlessly placing a trunk on the deck beside Hannah's uptilted one. "You, boy!" he ordered. "Give us a hand here! Place this trunk and bring those two still on the quay. This scrawny young'un can't do it."

The black man looked quickly toward his owner, a well-dressed, silver-haired gentleman, got a nod of permission and, with a good-natured wink for Hannah, went to finish her task.

Hannah ran ahead of him, grabbed her bundle, and threw the cloak over her arm. Then she watched in amazement as the man swung one of the trunks easily onto his shoulder and carried it up the gangplank. Hannah followed.

"I can't imagine what earthly good this one's going to be to us!" the mistress complained.

"Oh, shut up, Peg!" the master said. "She can wash dishes and scrub the floor and empty chamber pots, can't she? She can do all those things you think you're too good to do. I can get us a good strong boy to do the heavy lifting."

The mistress glared at him, then at Hannah. Suddenly, her gaze fell on the cloak Hannah carried over one arm.

"What's a stupid slave doing with a cloak like this?" she growled, jerking it away from Hannah and holding it up to the fading light. "If that ain't the best imported wool, I ain't never seen none! Did you steal this, girl?" She removed the dirty gray shawl around her shoulders and dropped it to the deck, then flung the cloak around her, stretching it across her bulk. She pranced across the deck and peered over the rail, trying to catch a glimpse of her reflection in the water.

"My former master gave it to me, ma'am," Hannah explained. "It belonged to my mistress, and she died, so he gave it to me. He said I would need something to keep me warm this winter."

"A likely story!" Mistress Weston snorted. "Who would give such a fine cloak to the likes of you? I'm sure you stole it. But you'll not profit from your ill-gotten gains, girl. The cloak is mine now!"

Hannah couldn't believe her ears. Surely no one could be so cruel! She knew Master Alex was right. She would need a warm cloak this winter, but most of all, she wanted the cloak because it had belonged to her beloved Mistress Annabelle. But what could she do about it? She belonged to Mistress

Weston now, like it or not, and apparently, so did her cloak! The sea air already held a chill, though, and she knew it would get worse as they sailed away from the land and into the open channel between Charleston and the Sea Islands.

"Begging your pardon, ma'am," she said, "but it is already January, and my dress is thin. How will I keep warm?"

Mistress Weston looked at her like she doubted her sanity. "Do you think I'll spend my time worrying about how you keep warm, girl?" she asked.

"No, ma'am, I reckon you won't," Hannah retorted, her anger getting the better of her judgment. "But I won't be much help to you if I'm shivering with cold so that I can't hold on to things or if I catch the lung fever and die, now will I?"

The mistress studied her. "Feisty little thing, ain't you?" she growled. Then she reached down, picked up the dirty shawl, and threw it at Hannah. "There! Wear that."

Hannah caught the shawl and held it between her thumb and forefinger. It smelled of woodsmoke, old bacon grease, and other things best left unknown.

"Well, what's the matter, girl?" Mistress Weston asked. "That shawl's kept me warm for a long time now, and it's certainly good enough for the likes of you!"

Hannah said nothing. She was determined not to wear the nasty thing until she could wash it. Her ma would have burned it! But she would have to use it because it was plain to see that Mistress Weston was not going to give back Mistress Annabelle's cloak.

"You'll sleep here and keep an eye on the baggage," Master Weston said. "There's no room for it in that tiny box below that they call a cabin." He started down some stairs cut into the deck, then turned back. "You can bring our breakfast to our cabin in the morning, young'un. Not too early," he added. "We'll rest while we can, for there'll be a plenty to do when we reach our destination!"

"But how will I fix break . . ." she began, but the master

35

and the mistress had disappeared down the steps.

Hannah sat down, leaning against one of the trunks, hugging her bundle to her, dreading the days ahead. How could she serve people who ordered her to do things and provided no means of doing them? What had she done to make these people despise her so? How she longed to go back to the days of serving sweet, gentle Mistress Annabelle! Or back to the carefree days she had known as the child of the head cook on Riceland Plantation, where Master Benson, though he had paid her little attention, had never treated her unkindly.

Then the thought came that she could not go back. There was no Mistress Annabelle to serve, and she was no longer the same Hannah who had played in the sand and the waves with Romy or gathered berries and flowers with her brothers and sisters on the island. She could read now. She could speak nearly perfect English. She knew how to be responsible for the comfort of another person. She was a different Hannah now.

Who was the Hannah that would serve the Westons, though? she wondered. Would she become a weary drudge who could see no farther than a pile of dirty dishes or muddy floors and nasty chamber pots? Where was the real Hannah? Would she ever find her amid all the changes? Who was she?

The sun was sinking into the sea on the horizon, but a sudden breeze filled the sails and she felt the boat shudder, then begin to pick up speed. The coast of South Carolina sped past, a blur in the growing darkness.

The wind that filled the sails cut right through her thin yellow dress. Hannah rubbed her bare arms below the short sleeves to chase away the chill. Then she opened her bundle, took out her nightshift, and wrapped it around her shoulders. It wasn't any thicker than her dress, but its meager warmth was welcome. Tomorrow maybe she could wash the filthy shawl and dry it in the wind as the boat sailed along. She wondered how long Mistress Weston had worn it, and if she had ever washed it.

How could she wash, though, with no tub and no soap? And how could she prepare breakfast without food to cook or a fireplace to cook it? The Westons had offered her nothing with which to do the chores they expected of her.

A fresh gust of wind cut straight through her, and Hannah looked around for shelter. Seeing a small space between two of the trunks, she wedged her way into it and worked a bag across each end to create a cramped, but somewhat protected sleeping area. Lying with her head propped up on one bag, she took her other dress out of her bundle and spread it over her. Somehow, she managed to fall asleep, dreaming fitfully of the islands and the tall, gray house in Charleston she had learned to love.

When she awoke at last to a thin, damp sunlight edging across the deck, it took a minute for her to realize where she was and why. Then it all came flooding back—the sorrow of having to leave Gray Gables, the harsh expectations of her new owners, Mistress Weston taking Mistress Annabelle's cloak that was supposed to belong to Hannah.

What is that awful smell? she wondered. Then she discovered that sometime during the night she had pulled Mistress Weston's shawl over her shivering body. She flung the smelly thing from her and crawled out from between the trunks.

The black man who had carried the trunks for her yesterday was cooking something in an iron skillet held over a three-legged kettle. As he lifted the skillet to fork bacon onto a tin plate, she moved closer and saw that the kettle held a bed of glowing coals nestled in sand. Beside this makeshift fireplace, for safety she reckoned, sat a bucket of water.

She watched the man break three eggs into the skillet and begin to flip the hot bacon grease over them until the yolks turned from yellow to pink, surrounded by a small island of white. Hannah's empty stomach rolled, and her mouth filled with saliva.

The man looked up. "Mawnin," he said, with a friendly

smile that exposed a missing tooth. "You wanna be usin' my utensils?"

"Why, thank you, sir," Hannah answered, "but I don't have anything to cook."

He shook his head. "I heard dem order you to fix breakfast, but dey didn't provide no food and no utensils? And I reckon you be gettin' what for if you doan bring it!" he grumbled, almost to himself. "Well, dis time we be foolin' 'em!"

He picked up a wicked-looking knife and began to slice strips from a large side of bacon and put them in the skillet. Then he carefully counted out six eggs.

"My master won't be carin'," he assured her, "if he ever be findin' out," he added with a wink. "Slaves done be havin' to survive, anyways dey can, missy. And de slyer we be, de better! If dere be time, I be tellin' you about Big John and how he be outwittin' his greedy master every time!"

Hannah felt his words roll over her like a wave of sunwarmed sea water over bare feet. "You're Gullah!" she exclaimed happily.

He flashed her a wide grin as he reached for a big pot and poured coffee into a tin mug. "Yes'um, I be Gullah," he agreed, "straight from a rice plantation on St. Simon's Island. Samson, dey calls me. But how duz you be knowin' Gullah? Yo' speech be white-folks proper!"

It was Hannah's turn to grin. "I be workin' on it to please my former mistress. But I be Gullah, for sure, from Sunrise Island," she declared. "I know all about Big John and Br'er Rabbit and dere sly ways."

"I be pleased to be makin' your acquaintance, Miss . . ."

"Hannah," she supplied, shaking the huge hand he held out to her.

"Don't let yo' bacon burn, Miss Hannah!" he warned, and she hurried to turn it, then went to the trunks to hunt for the dishes Mistress Weston had been so concerned about the day before. But the trunks were locked, and seeing her predicament, Samson handed her two tin plates, two forks, and two tin mugs from the trunk he had been carrying before he was sent to help her.

"Eat yo' breakfas' fust, missy," Samson advised, "or you likely won't be havin' any, not with dat pair! Help yo'sef to de coffee," he added. He picked up his plate and mug and headed for the stairs, whistling through the gap in his teeth.

"Thank you, Samson!" she called. He nodded his head without looking back.

Hannah took up the bacon and broke eggs into the grease. Following Samson's advice, she quickly ate two eggs and two thick pieces of bacon, then rinsed the plate in the bucket of water. She filled both plates, poured coffee into the mugs and, juggling all of it, followed Samson below deck.

The big man was just coming out of one of the cabins, and she assumed the other one held the Westons. She knocked on the door with her foot. "Breakfast, Master, Mistress!" she called.

The door swung open, and the master's bloodshot eyes peered at her, then at the plates of food. "Where's the biscuits?" he grumbled, reaching for the mugs.

"Sir, you gave me no provisions. I was forced to borrow these. If you will open your trunks and give me food and utensils, I can do better next time."

He glared at her, then turned and carried the coffee mugs into the room. He returned, grabbed the plates, and shut the door in her face without another word.

"Did he think I wanted to come into that smelly old cabin with him and the mistress?" Hannah muttered to herself as she made her way back up the steep stairs to the deck. She didn't think either of the Westons had ever had a bath or washed their clothes!

Ma insisted that all of her children take a bath every Saturday night, whether they needed it or not! Ma wanted them to be shiny clean to attend services at the Praise House on Sunday.

Hannah felt a fresh wave of homesickness wash over her. She missed the Gullah services in the Praise House on Sunrise Island, with the honeysuckle twined around the live oak trees outside sending its sweet smell inside the small wooden building. She missed Elder Jems lining out the songs so all could know the words, and old Grandpa Mason calling for the tune in either short or long meter.

Then, after they had sung and prayed, Elder Jems would read the Scriptures, interrupted often by shouts of "hallelujah!" or "amen!" Sometimes he told them stories of Adam and Eve, or Samson and Delilah, or the little baby Jesus born in a cows' stall.

Twice a year, there were baptisms. Just last June, her sister Esther had given herself to the Lord and been baptized in the creek on a Sunday at ebb tide so the receding water would carry away her sins.

Most of all, Hannah reckoned she missed the "ring shouts," when, at the end of a service, the congregation would shuffle around in a circle to the rhythm of three leaders' clapping hands, singing at the tops of their voices, and now and then throwing in a little dance.

She hadn't attended a worship service since she was brought to Charleston. Mistress Annabelle had not been able to leave her room to go to church, and Hannah had not had the nerve to ask if she could go alone. She had attended the mistress' funeral at the big stone church on the corner. Master Alex had given her permission to go with Lettie and sit in the balcony with the other black people. But that had been a sad occasion, not at all like the happy times she had known in the Gullah services.

She reckoned worship in the tall, dignified churches of Charleston wouldn't be the same as at the Praise House, anyway. When she passed one of those huge buildings of stone or brick on her way to the market or the wharf, she never heard any loud singing or shouting or any laughter coming from inside them.

Would she ever be in a Gullah Praise House again? she wondered sadly. Were there any churches at all where they were going? "Oh, how can I bear going off to some awful heathen wilderness with these awful people?" she said aloud, tears threatening.

The days went by, though, and they traveled on, leaving the boat to ride overland in a coach pulled by horses, then boarding a flatboat to float down the Monongahela and the Ohio Rivers. Finally, they landed at a little town called Limestone, a place Samson called, ". . . de berry top of Kentucky!"

While they waited there for Master Weston to decide where he wanted to go, a man came riding up to Limestone from the south and offered to sell them a tavern in Frankfort.

"It's the capital of Kentucky, you know," Hannah heard the master say to the mistress. "And it's built right on the banks of the river. The town ain't big, but river traffic will bring a steady flow of customers right to our door!"

"I don't like buying something sight unseen," the mistress complained. "It's like buying a pig in a poke. You never know if you've got a bad bargain until it's too late!"

The master, though, shared a jug of liquor with the man, and the tavern was bought. Immediately, he began to buy up supplies and arranged for two horses and a wagon to transport them down the Wilderness Road to the Kentucky River, where they would take a flatboat the rest of the way. By the time they were ready to go, it was well into April.

"You take care, missy Hannah," Samson called, as they loaded the Weston's belongings into the wagon. "My master and me be stayin' here for a while, but I 'spects you and me be meetin' up somewhere by and by."

"Good-bye, Samson!" she called, climbing into the back of the wagon with the trunks and supplies. She wondered if he was right and they would meet again. She felt very lonely as the horses pulled the wagon into the road and headed south.

Chapter Five

"There it is!" Master Weston called out. "Pull in at the landing there!" he ordered the boatmen.

Hannah looked up the muddy riverbank to where it began to level off at the top. She could see three buildings above them. Was the Westons' new tavern that tall brick house barely visible through the blooming redbud trees? Was it the small stone cottage to the right? Surely it wasn't that log building between them! Who would want to stay in that squat, ugly place?

As the boatmen eased the flatboat out of the current into the calmer water near the landing, Hannah saw that someone had cut narrow steps into the steep mud bank all the way to the top and placed beside them a wooden handrail made of tree limbs still covered with bark.

As soon as the boat was tied to the rough wooden dock that jutted into the water, Mistress Weston hopped onto the dock and stood looking at those steps.

"A prime property, indeed!" she muttered. "Weston, I'm going to kill you! The way you carried on about this place, I thought we were moving into a palace!" Mistress Weston said.

Master Weston ignored her complaints, continuing to give orders about unloading the trunks and bags.

Hannah picked up a bag from the dock and followed her mistress up the steps, holding carefully to the unpeeled rail as she climbed.

Above her, the ugly cabin loomed, almost on the edge of the riverbank, its logs sagging in the middle so that it seemed to be held erect by the huge stone chimneys at either end. Beyond it, stood an equally run-down log building that Hannah thought must be a stable, for there was a hitching post beside it.

Mistress Weston pulled the latch on the back door, and it swung open slowly on creaky hinges, as though reluctant to expose what lay within. The mistress hesitated, then stepped inside. Hannah heard her groan.

Quickly, Hannah followed. She set the bag down and waited for her eyes to adjust to the dimness.

She was in a small entry with three doorways and a stairway opening out of it. To Hannah's right, a narrow hall ran beside the stairs to a storage space with empty, dusty shelves.

To her left, an opening led into what she reckoned was a kitchen. It stretched all the way to the front of the building, where a window looked out onto the dirt-paved street. A crude table occupied most of the room. The end wall held a huge fireplace taller than she was, outfitted with a swinging crane to hold kettles over the fire and a spit for roasting meat. Beside the fireplace was an oven built into the wall, and above it, extending from the half-log mantel, were wooden pegs for hanging utensils.

The room directly in front of her took up the rest of the first floor, ending with a fireplace as big as the one in the kitchen, but without the cooking tools. Only a pile of long-dead ashes lay inside it. There was a door in the center of the front wall, flanked by windows on either side, which were the only sources of light. A rough wooden bar extended nearly down the length of the back wall, and three long tables with benches filled the rest of the room. The wide floorboards were caked with dried mud, and everything was covered with dust and spiderwebs.

Hannah sighed as she considered the hours of scrubbing ahead of her. She wouldn't be likely to have any help, either. Would the Westons even supply her with the tools to do the job?

"Well, girl, you've got your work cut out for you," the mistress said, as though she took great pleasure in making Hannah work hard. "I'm going upstairs to see the bedrooms."

"Where do you want me to start, mistress?" Hannah asked.

"This room must be made ready to welcome patrons immediately," Mistress Weston said. "We have to get the money flowing. Then the bedrooms must be prepared for travelers." Her voice faded as she disappeared through the back doorway. Hannah heard her footsteps mounting the stairs, then pacing back and forth overhead. Soon she heard them descending the stairs again.

"There's beds up there, at least," she said, coming back into the room. "Three of them in the one big room, and one each in the little end rooms. One of those will be mine and Weston's. We'll save the other one for families, and the big room will make a dormitory for single travelers. It's a good thing I brought all my linens and covers from the inn in Georgia!"

"Yes, ma'am," Hannah answered, for want of something better to say.

"I can't imagine why Weston was so set on coming here!" the mistress muttered. "We'll likely starve to death in this filthy hole!"

Hannah almost laughed aloud. She doubted that Peg Weston would recognize filth if she fell in it!

Master Weston came into the room and dropped the other bag on the floor by the bar. Two men carrying trunks followed him. They set the trunks down and went out. In minutes, they were back bringing the other trunk and the bags of provisions. Hannah saw the master drop some coins into their hands, and they left. Soon she heard the head boatman chanting orders as they pulled back into the current and headed downstream.

Mistress Weston was already opening trunks and pulling out tools and supplies. Before long, Hannah was at work, sweeping spiderwebs from the open rafters, cleaning out the fireplace, scrubbing the bar and the furniture with lye soap. The pieces with bark on them were difficult to scrub, but she gave it a good try with a brush. Then she took the brush to the dried mud on the wide boards of the floor. By the end of the day, the big room was as clean as it was ever going to be.

Hannah stood up, rubbing her back. Then she looked down. Most of the dirt, it seemed, had been transferred to her yellow dress. She didn't know if she could ever get it clean again! But she had managed to get the filth out of Mistress Weston's hand-me-down shawl. Surely she could save the dress that Ma had put so much time into making pretty for her!

The master came in with an armload of wood. "This place needs a good drying out," he said, laying kindling to start a fire and taking out his tinderbox. But the smoke from his fire refused to go up the chimney, curling into the room from the top of the fireplace opening. He swore and stomped outside. Hannah soon heard him on the roof, swearing and poking at the chimney. A chunk of mud fell, shattered in the fireplace, and scattered over the hearth. Hannah ran to sweep it up before careless steps could mash it into her clean hearth, noting thankfully that the smoke now was going straight up the chimney.

She looked up as Mistress Weston came in from the store-room, where she had been arranging their supplies for the tavern. Hannah couldn't help wondering if she had dusted the shelves first.

"Finished, are you, girl?" she asked.

"Yes, ma'am," Hannah answered, looking around the clean room with satisfaction. *I've done a good job,* she thought. Surely the mistress would praise her.

"Then get in the kitchen and start supper!" Mistress Weston ordered, digging in one of the trunks for bed linens. "It's nearly bedtime! Tomorrow you'll need to start and finish earlier so we can eat at a decent time."

Hannah stared at her until the mistress looked up. "What are you lookin' at, girl?" she snapped.

Hannah wanted to say, "Not much!" as she and her brothers used to say to each other when they wanted to tease. She didn't dare, though. "Nothing, ma'am," was the best she could manage.

The mistress stared at her suspiciously for a moment, then went back to her trunk. Hannah hurried out of the room before the woman could realize what she meant by that answer.

She went into the storeroom and sliced meat from a hog shoulder. The mistress had said they would save the hams to serve in the tavern. But Hannah knew shoulder could be good. Her ma could make it taste nearly like ham. She'd have to fry this, though, for there wasn't time to boil it slowly with herbs.

Where has the mistress put the potatoes? she wondered, turning to the sacks beneath the still-dusty shelves. As she had thought, the mistress hadn't bothered to clean them before putting the supplies on them.

Oh, well, Hannah thought, *that's a job for another day.* She was glad, though, that her ma and Lettie had taught her how to keep house, as she put the meat into a skillet and buried potatoes in the ashes of the master's fire. There wasn't time to start one in the kitchen fireplace tonight, not with the mistress already complaining about the lateness of their supper.

The mistress came down from the bedroom and inspected what she was doing; then, without comment, she stirred up a batch of cornbread, put it to bake in a covered skillet, and set a pot of coffee on to boil.

When the food was done, Hannah filled two plates with the meat, potatoes, and bread, and poured coffee into two mugs and set them at the end of one of the tables. She placed two forks beside them. She filled another plate for herself and carried it into the kitchen, as she had been taught.

She had just finished eating when Mistress Weston called, "After you wash the dishes, Hannah, you can bed down in the storeroom. Tomorrow, you can clean the kitchen and start on the upstairs. I'll take care of our room myself," she added graciously.

"Yes, ma'am!" Hannah said, going into the big room to

gather up the empty plates and mugs and carry them into the kitchen. When she heard two sets of footsteps mounting the stairs, she plunged the dishes into a kettle of cold water. She was too tired to wait for water to heat over the fire, so she scrubbed the plates with her bare fingers and dried them on a dishtowel from one of the trunks. Maybe nobody would notice that they were still smeared a little with grease. Tomorrow, she promised herself, she would do better.

Wearily, she went into the storeroom, and looked around for some way to make a bed, but the windowless room was pitch dark. All at once, she felt as though a "hant" was there, just behind her, waiting to pounce! She turned and ran into the big room with its light from the fireplace. She rummaged in a trunk for the mistress' supply of candles. Lighting one from the fireplace, she carried it into the storeroom and held it high so she could see.

Pushed together, the bags of meal, flour, and sugar would make a pretty good mattress. But they weighed 100 pounds each, and in the morning, she would have to put them back where she had found them before the mistress saw what she had done.

Suddenly tired of trying so hard to please the mistress, almost always without success, she walked resolutely back into the big room. She took one of the mistress' precious covers from the trunk and spread it on the clean floor. *I will sleep here before the fire and be warm for once,* she thought rebelliously. With a sassy grin, she plucked a pillow from the trunk and added it to her bed.

Hannah blew out the candle and lay down, pulling her clean shawl over her. Her tired bones had barely eased into rest before she was asleep.

* * *

"What are you doing here! And with my cover and pillow!" the mistress screamed. She snatched the pillow and tugged to get the cover from under Hannah.

Hannah jumped up, her eyes wide with confusion. Then her deliberate defiance of the mistress' orders returned to her memory, and fear crept down her spine.

"I told you to sleep in the storeroom, girl!" Mistress Weston said through clenched teeth, and Hannah's head jerked back with the force of her slap.

Hannah's hand flew to her stinging cheek. She had never been slapped before! Ma had switched them now and then, or paddled their bottoms with the butter paddle, but never had she slapped them! Even Miss Lettie, mean as she talked sometimes, had never laid a hand on her. Hannah felt tears welling in her eyes and turned her back to keep the mistress from seeing them. It was embarrassing to make such a baby of herself. She was twelve years old! She had meant to put her bed away and have breakfast going before her owners were up.

The mistress grabbed Hannah's arm and swung her around. "Don't you dare turn your back on me, you wretched brat!" she yelled, slapping her again.

"Mistress Weston, I be sorry!" Hannah stammered. "The storeroom was dark and dusty, and I be cold, so I . . ."

"So you helped yourself to my cover and my pillow!" the mistress screamed.

"Where's my breakfast?" the master bellowed, coming through the back door. "Why, there's not even a fire going!" He went over to the fireplace and began to poke at the nearly dead embers, putting kindling on them and fanning them with a bellows.

"This lazy good-for-nothing thinks she'll sleep all mornin', I reckon," his wife informed him, "and on my pillow and cover! Can you imagine? A slave using my things?" She shuddered, as though Hannah had contaminated them.

"All right, Peg," the master said wearily. "You've slapped her around. Now, let her get my breakfast! We've got work to do." He rummaged in one of the trunks and brought out a jug, pulled the cork from it, and took several swallows. He wiped his mouth on the back of his hand. "I want this place open for business by tomorrow evening," he added, sitting down at the table with the jug before him.

"Cook in here, girl," the mistress ordered. "We ain't got time for you to make a fire in the kitchen. Just fry some meat and eggs and heat up the cornbread left from supper. I'll fix the coffee. Yours ain't fit to drink."

Hannah's thoughts were whirling. Her face stung with the woman's slaps, but inside she ached with longing to be at home with her ma on Sunrise Island or back at Gray Gables, even with the sharp-tongued Lettie. Nobody had ever treated her this way! But what could she do? She belonged to these people as surely as this tavern or the furniture in it did. A new understanding of just what it meant to be a slave came over her.

I could run away, she thought. But where could she go? She had no means of travel, no horse or mule, no carriage or wagon. She had no boat. On foot, they would surely catch her, and she knew that the punishment for runaways often was death.

By the time she had breakfast on the table, Hannah's thin face had swollen until she looked like a squirrel with hickory nuts in its cheeks. All morning, as she scrubbed at the dirt in the kitchen, she worked to the rhythm of a dull throbbing pain.

The mistress had yet to give her a kind word, but she never had hit her before. Of course, Hannah never had defied her that way before, either. *I will never defy her again!* she promised herself. If she couldn't get away from her, she would have to do her best to please her mistress.

The master didn't seem to care much what she did, so long as the mistress was pleased and he could have his jug. But he certainly wouldn't do anything to defend her, either. That was as plain as this awful throbbing in her jaw.

"Start a fire in this fireplace, girl," the mistress said, coming into the kitchen after the noon meal. "I'm goin' to show you how to roast a spit of meat. Call me when the fire is ready." With that, she left the room.

Hannah hurried to do as she was told, praying the fire would start with little trouble. When the flames were roaring up the chimney, she called the mistress back to the kitchen.

"That won't do at all!" she exclaimed. "Don't you know anything, girl? The fire has to be burning steadily so it will roast the meat, not burn it to a cinder! I'm going upstairs and lie down. Call me when it's ready, and not before!"

Hannah looked at the roaring flames. There was nothing she could do now but let it burn down of its own accord.

Suddenly she had to get out of this place. Throwing her shawl around her shoulders, she ran out the back door.

Chapter Six

Hannah stood outside the back door, looking down toward the river. *If I could just get on that old river's back and ride it to the sea, would I float right up to the wharf at Charleston?* she wondered.

Her life at Gray Gables had been good, in spite of the work and her bouts of homesickness. Mistress Annabelle truly had cared about her. Hannah had been almost like a member of the family. Mistress Annabelle was gone, though. Likely, Mr. Alex was gone, too. She had nobody in Charleston now.

Maybe I would wash ashore on one of the Sea Islands, she thought, *right up on the beach.* And while she was dreaming, she might as well imagine that she washed up on Sunrise Island where she could go straight home.

Hannah wondered what her ma and brothers and sisters would be doing right now. She put up a hand to wipe away a tear and winced in pain as she touched her swollen cheek. Suddenly she wondered about Ruth and Naomi. Had her older sisters been sold into good situations with kind owners like Mistress Annabelle and Master Alex? Or did they, too, bear the marks of a master's or mistress' anger? And Mark and Luke—how did they fare?

She sighed. She hoped all of them were in situations better than hers. As for riding the river back home, even if she had a boat, there was no place to go. She had been sold. She didn't belong on the islands anymore. She no longer had her own little room in the attic at Gray Gables. She had a corner of the cold, dark storeroom where she could sleep. Was there no pleasant place in all the world now that she could call her own?

She looked to her left toward the small stone house she had seen from the boat yesterday. Someone must live there, for the grasses of the lawn had been trimmed and a small garden had been started on either side of the path to the back door. Already, the green sprouts of onions and peas were flourishing in the April sun in the bed nearest her, and some other green plants were coming through the ground in the far bed.

She saw a tall white man come out the back door, followed closely by a stocky black man. They stood on the path between the garden beds, the black man listening intently to what the white man was saying. The black man nodded, walked to the far side of the house, and disappeared around the corner. The white man turned and went back inside.

It wouldn't do for her to go wandering over that way, Hannah decided, turning to survey the property on her right.

From here, the tall brick house she had glimpsed from the boat was nearly hidden in a tangle of trees and shrubbery. She walked over to the untrimmed hedge and pushed some of its branches aside so she could see into the yard.

The three-story house sat farther back from the riverbank than the tavern or the stone house, its lawn descending to the river in terraces. Hannah thought that it must have been beautiful once, with its flower beds and small stone benches and fountains connected by winding brick walks. Now the dried brown stems of past years' flowers and weeds choked the new-green shoots of spring, and grasses grew between the bricks.

What was that strange smell, that kind of musty odor? It smelled like . . . like the stable on Riceland where they kept the horses and their harnesses. Yes, that was it! It was the odor of old, dried horse sweat. Was there a stable nearby?

Hannah pushed through the hedge and the odor grew stronger. She plucked a leaf and rubbed it between her thumb and forefinger, then sniffed. There it was—the odor of horse sweat! What kind of bushes were these, anyway? They surrounded the property.

She crept across the lawn to the side of the house and edged along it to the front. Here, only a narrow brick walk separated the house from the dirt track that served as a street. There was no lawn and no hedge.

Not wanting to be caught prowling around the house, Hannah walked to the street, passed the house, then ducked back into the yard on the other side. Keeping within the cover of the bushes and trees, she made her way to where the lawn dropped off to a lower level.

A few feet from the bottom of six brick steps, she could see a white stone surrounded by more of the "horse sweat" shrubs. Descending the steps, she followed the grass-free brick walk to the right and entered the enclosure through an opening at the side. The space inside the hedge held a border of yellow and white flowers. There were no weeds or last-year's stems inside the hedge.

Hannah walked around to the front of the stone. "Miriam Elizabeth Crenshaw," it read, "1790-1798." Someone had placed a fresh bouquet of purple violets at the bottom of the stone.

It was the grave of a little girl—she quickly counted on her fingers—eight years old when she died. She counted again. She would have been eleven now, just a year younger than Hannah. *What happened to her?* she wondered. *And why is she buried all alone here on the riverbank? Does her family still live in the brick house? Or have they moved on, like Mr. Alex?* But someone had been here recently to tend the grave and bring flowers.

A door slammed. Hannah wasn't sure if it came from the tavern or from the stone house, but she realized that she had been gone too long. If the mistress caught her here, she was sure to get another slapping.

Quickly, she crossed the lawn and slipped back through the hedge. She was inside the back entry before she heard Mistress Weston calling her as she came down the stairs.

"The neighbors who live in that stone house over there

have a garden," Hannah babbled. "Would you want me to be putting out a garden, mistress? We always had a kitchen garden at Riceland," she finished breathlessly.

"In due time, we will plant a garden," Mistress Weston answered. "Is the fire ready to cook meat now?"

Hannah ran into the kitchen. "Yes, ma'am, I believe it is," she called back. Then Samson's advice about a slave outwitting his owner came back to her. "Of course, I don't know much about cooking meat, mistress. I'll need you to show me. Then I can do it just the way you want it done."

Mistress Weston came into the room, throwing Hannah a suspicious look. Hannah kept her eyes as wide and innocent as Big John or Br'er Rabbit surely ever did. Somehow, though, being sly didn't make her feel good. She had always answered Ma truthfully when she was caught in some mischief. She didn't like being sneaky. She reckoned Samson was right, though—a slave had to survive any way she could.

"Pay attention now, girl," Mistress Weston ordered, swinging the spit away from the fire and shoving it right through the middle of a ham. She swung it back over the deeply glowing embers and stepped back. "If you see it start to burn, swing it over a little, away from the hottest part of the fire," she instructed. "Back in Georgia, our tavern was famous for our hams. I don't aim for this one to be any different, though who will come to this muddy hole of a town, I can't imagine!"

"Do you want me to put some sweet potatoes in the ashes and fry some meat for supper, ma'am?" Hannah asked. "I reckon it will be hours before that ham is done."

The mistress nodded. "It will need to roast all night. I'll make the biscuits," she said then. "Weston says your bread ain't fit for the dogs, and I reckon he's right!"

"I have not been taught to make bread, ma'am," Hannah explained. "Our cook, Lettie, always made the bread at the DuVane's, and my ma always made it at home. I reckon she would have taught me someday, if I hadn't been sold. But Ma liked making bread, and everybody said her bread couldn't be beat." Hannah's mouth watered as she remembered the smell of Ma's bread baking on the hearth. She swallowed. "I reckon it's a special talent. Maybe you could teach me, mistress?"

Mistress Weston threw her another suspicious look, but Hannah's eyes were wide and innocent. *Well, I really do want to know how to make bread,* she thought, but she doubted that this woman's skills were up to her ma's or even grumpy old Lettie's. The mistress seemed pleased, though, and Hannah silently thanked Samson for his advice. Maybe she and this mistress would be able to get along, after all. Maybe if she treated Mistress Weston with respect, she would return the favor.

By the time supper was ready, Hannah had had her first lesson in making biscuits. Not even the master complained. In fact, he ate five! Then, he picked up his jug and settled down in front of the fire while Hannah and the mistress cleaned up the dishes and the kitchen.

Finally, the mistress went into the big room, roused her husband from his drunken stupor, and sent him to bed. In a moment, she came back into the room and tossed Hannah a ragged quilt. "There's your cover, girl," she said. "And, remember, the storeroom is where you sleep."

Encouraged by the unusual gesture of kindness, Hannah said, "But, ma'am, it's so cold and dark in there, and the dust makes me cough. Could I please sleep in front of one of the fireplaces? I promise to be up and have my pallet put away before ..."

The mistress' cold stare cut off Hannah's words. "How dare you argue with me!"

"Oh, no, ma'am!" Hannah stammered. "I don't be arguin'! I just thought ..."

"Thinkin' ain't your job, girl," she said sharply. "It's what gets you in trouble."

"Yes, ma'am," Hannah answered meekly, looking at the floor. *Oh, Samson, what do I do now?* she wondered. She just couldn't sleep in that storeroom! She'd smother in the thick, dusty dark!

"I want you up before daylight, with the fire going in the kitchen and breakfast started before we come down," the mistress added. She turned and left the room, and Hannah heard her footsteps on the stairs.

She banked the ashes over the fire so it would not go out, and picking up the candle from the table, went into the storeroom and set the candle on the bottom shelf. She checked to see if the meal sack was securely tied, then pushed it over on the floor and spread the cover below it. She grabbed her shawl from the wooden peg by the door, wrapped it around her, blew out the candle, and lay down. She pillowed her head on the meal sack, and pulled half the cover over her.

Hannah covered her head with the cover to shut out the dust, trying not to cough, trying not to think about the narrow, windowless room or the heavy darkness pressing in on her like a grave.

Suddenly, she remembered the small grave she had discovered next door that afternoon. Who was the child who lay buried there? What had happened to Miriam Elizabeth Crenshaw?

Then she remembered something Elder Jems often said in funerals at the Praise House: "Beloved, only de body, de discarded house of de soul, goes to de grave. De soul of dis fine Christian be gone straight to God!"

Where is little Miriam Elizabeth? she wondered. She hoped she was in a place with beautiful flowers blooming and birds singing. She hoped she was in a place of light and fresh air.

Hannah jumped up, grabbed her cover, and ran into the kitchen. She simply could not stay in that storeroom, no matter what the mistress said, not even if she came downstairs and beat her for it!

She spread out the cover before the fireplace and lay down. The glow of the banked embers made her feel better immediately. But every creak of the old house made her jump, afraid the mistress was up and about to descend upon her. And, afraid that she would again oversleep, she slept hardly at all.

It was still black outside the window when she got up, rolled up her cover, and stowed it back in the storeroom beside the again properly placed sack of meal. And she had breakfast nearly ready when she heard the mistress' feet hit the floor upstairs.

Just as the sun crept over the windowsill, there was a knock at the front door. The mistress looked at Hannah. "Take up those biscuits, girl, while I answer the door," she ordered.

Hannah heard her invite someone to come in and have a seat. She came back into the kitchen, her face flushed with excitement. "We have our first customer!" she announced. "Take him a plate of ham, eggs, and biscuits, girl. I'll get the coffee and some of that grape jelly from the storeroom. We want word to get out quickly about what a good table we spread here!" she added in a loud whisper.

Hannah hurried to fix the plate of food and carry it into the big room, where she found a small man dressed in buckskin shirt and pants seated at the table nearest the fireplace. His hair and beard were badly in need of trimming, and his hands needed a good washing with lye soap.

He folded a piece of ham inside the biscuit, chewed hungrily, swallowed, then grunted with satisfaction. He took a big drink of the mistress' coffee, and sighed happily. When he had eaten everything and sopped up the egg yolk with his last biscuit, he called for more. Hannah refilled his plate, but the mistress took it from her and carried it to him.

"We had a good tavern in Georgia," she said when she came back to the kitchen carrying the empty plate and mug. "The Brass Lion, we called it. And that's what we're going to call this one."

Hannah swallowed laughter. She didn't want to antagonize Mistress Weston when she was in such a good mood. But there wasn't any kind of lion in the building, and certainly not a brass one!

"I will have a sign painted, as soon as I can find a painter. We will hang it over the front door, so people will know we are open for business. This man was just passing through on his way to Virginia, and the flatboat captain told him we were here. But there will be other travelers, and people from right here in Frankfort will come. We just need to get the word out. Weston will have to see if there's a local newspaper where we can place an ad."

Hannah poured hot water into a kettle, shaved some lye soap into it, and began to wash dishes. The mistress hung a kettle of water on the crane and threw some meat into it.

"Cut these potatoes and onions up into the soup," the mistress ordered. "I will see what else I can find to go into it. Then, if customers come for the noon meal, we will be ready. We need to get the bedrooms ready, too, in case we have travelers who need lodging."

Hannah did as she was told, then went upstairs to finish cleaning the big room that held three beds. When she had finished, she began on the little room the mistress was saving to rent to families who would not want to spend the night in a room full of strange men.

She served the noon meal to the Westons, but no customers came to eat with them.

"We just need to get the word out," the mistress repeated.

The master grunted, rubbed his bloodshot eyes, and reached for his jug.

The mistress beat him to it, setting the jug on a shelf behind the bar. "No more of that until you go see if there's a newspaper in this town, and find out what an ad will cost," she said. "And see if you can locate a painter to fix us a sign. I want it to read: 'The Brass Lion, the best food and drink west of the mountains!'"

Muttering under his breath, the master went to the storeroom for his coat, and still muttering, went out.

Hannah finished the small bedroom and made all the beds. She heard the mistress come upstairs and go into her room. It was time for her afternoon nap. Hannah knew what she would do with her few moments of freedom today! She would go back to visit the grave next door.

Chapter Seven

Hannah studied the tall brick house carefully. There was no sign of anyone there. Quickly, she made her way down to the second level of the lawn and sat down beside the gravestone.

Below her, the river swept by on its way to the sea, but it would be best if she didn't think about the sea, or islands in the sea, or her family on one of them. She missed her brothers and sisters and her ma terribly. It hadn't been so bad when she was at Gray Gables because she had felt the DuVanes were her friends, as well as her owners, and she had been busy learning so many new, exciting things. Here, she had no one who cared about her, no family, and no friends.

If Miriam Elizabeth Crenshaw had lived, would we have become friends? she wondered. They would have been almost the same age, and they would have lived right next door to each other. Of course, Mistress Weston made sure she didn't have much time to herself. And, most likely, Miriam Elizabeth had been a little white girl, and Hannah was a slave. Still, she sometimes had played with the children of Master Benson's visitors. That had not been a problem on Riceland Plantation.

"What are you doing on that grave?"

The shrill voice made Hannah jump guiltily, though, so far as she knew, she had done nothing wrong. She looked up, straight into a pair of piercing brown eyes in a face distorted with anger. Instinctively, Hannah threw up her arm to protect her head.

"I asked you what you are doing on that grave!" the woman repeated.

"Why, ma'am, I'm just sitting here thinking, I reckon," Hannah stammered. "This little girl would be about my age if she . . ."

"She'd be eleven," the woman cut her off crisply. "She was my only grandchild, the child of my only son, but she lived with me. Her mother died when she was born."

Like Mistress Annabelle, Hannah thought.

"What happened to Miriam Elizabeth, ma'am?" Hannah asked, her curiosity getting the better of her fear.

"She died," the woman answered curtly. "And I am very particular about her grave. I'd rather you did not come here again."

"Yes, ma'am," Hannah replied. "I was just looking for a place to be alone and think, and I found her grave, and I began to wonder if we might have been friends had she still lived here next door to me."

"I assume, then, that you belong to the tavern keepers?"

"Yes, ma'am," she answered again, getting up to go. As she went through the gap in the hedge, she turned back. "Ma'am, would you be angry if I brought some flowers to Miriam Elizabeth now and then? I promise not to disturb her grave in any way. It's just that I'm so . . ." All at once, Hannah began to cry, big tears running down her face and dropping off her chin into the grass. She was embarrassed and ashamed, but once the tears had started, she couldn't seem to make them stop.

"Why, child!" the woman exclaimed. "What is it? Come here!" she demanded.

Hannah looked up to see that only concern showed on the woman's face now. She offered her handkerchief for the tears. Hannah shook her head, wiping her face on the hem of her dress.

"Are those bruises on your face, child?" the woman asked, peering at her closely. "Are you mistreated by the tavern keepers? I realize that you must be their slave, an institution I don't care much for, anyway. But there's no excuse for mistreatment of one's servants, whether they be slave or free. I will have a talk with your owners."

Hannah shook her head. "Oh, please, ma'am, don't! It would just make it worse. Anyway, I don't mind the slappings so much. It's just that my family is so far away, and I have no friends here, and . . ."

"You're lonely," the lady finished for her. "You are so lonely that you want to make friends with a little dead girl."

Hannah nodded miserably.

"She would have been your friend," the woman said softly, looking down at the stone. "She loved everything and everybody alive." Then Hannah saw a kind of shiver pass over her, and she straightened her shoulders. "I am Rachel Crenshaw," she introduced herself. "And what is your name?"

"Hannah. I am named for the woman in the Bible who gave her little son to God," she answered proudly.

"I gave my whole family to Him," Mrs. Crenshaw said, with a bitter smile. "Or perhaps I should say, He took them. Had I had any choice in the matter, they would still be here."

"Yes, ma'am," Hannah said, for want of something better to say.

"Well, Hannah, I too am very lonely. Come into the house with me, and we will have some tea and a nice talk," Mrs. Crenshaw suggested.

Hannah stared at her in amazement. Unless she had misunderstood, she—a slave girl—had just been invited to tea by the mistress of a fine house! She threw a worried glance toward the tavern. "I'm afraid I'd better be getting back," she refused reluctantly. "When my mistress gets up from her afternoon nap, she will expect me to be there, starting supper."

"Yes, of course," Mrs. Crenshaw said. "I forgot that your time is not your own. But perhaps another day, then, when your mistress first lies down to rest?"

Hannah studied the sad, dark eyes and the lined face. "I would like that, ma'am," she said, feeling a little less lonely as she hurried across the lawn to the back door of the tavern.

She pushed open the door, and her heart sank, for there stood Mistress Weston, a fist planted firmly on each hip.

"Where have you been, girl?" she snarled. "Here it is past four o'clock, and supper not even thought about yet! And what gives you the idea you can go roaming about at will? It may be that you don't have enough to do to keep you busy. I'll see what I can do about that!"

Oh, Samson, what do I do now? Hannah wondered. Just when she had somewhere to go and someone to be with, her free time was being taken away!

"I'll start supper right away, mistress," she promised, trying to edge past her into the kitchen.

"You think that's all of it, do you?" Mistress Weston said. "You little wretch! I'll teach you to go gallavantin' off when there's chores to be done!"

Hannah saw the slap coming and ducked, but the woman's big hand caught her on the side of the head and she reeled with the impact. The next slap landed on the painful remains of yesterday's slapping. She wanted to hit back, to push and shove and kick. But she belonged to this woman, like a dog or a mule. "Get in that kitchen and get supper started!" Mistress Weston ordered. "We may even have customers tonight."

Hannah stumbled into the kitchen. Her head spun, and she leaned against the rock of the fireplace to keep from falling. She was too miserable for tears. Would she have to endure this kind of treatment for the rest of her life? How could she?

The back door opened with a bang against the entry wall, and she heard Master Weston shout, "Peg, I've bought us a horse and cart, and come see what else!"

Hannah crept over to the doorway, then gasped in surprise. With Master Weston was a black boy whose bulk nearly filled the entry. He was staring down at the floor, like there was something very interesting about those old rough planks.

"This is Bo," Master Weston said. "He may be a little weak in the thinking department, but he's strong enough to do whatever we need him to do. He can cut and carry wood for the fireplaces, fetch water, tote supplies. He may even scrub floors for you, girl!" he said to Hannah with a grin.

"Hummph!" Mistress Weston grunted. "This one ain't gettin' help with chores! It appears to me she's already got too much time on her hands."

Bo looked up at her from dull brown eyes that gave hardly a flicker of recognition that she was there. Hannah had the feeling that whatever treatment he received from the Westons wouldn't be any worse than he had known before, and she felt sorry for him.

"Come on, boy," the master said. "I'll show you the woodpile and the best way to get to the river to get water. There ain't a well here, but I'm thinking on having one dug." His voice died away as they went outside.

Mistress Weston didn't object to Bo's carrying the wood for Hannah's supper fire, and Hannah was grateful for his help so she could get on with the cooking.

When Hannah filled a plate of meat and potatoes and handed it to Bo, he hunched down in the corner and ate every bite, then licked the plate clean. She knew better than to offer him a second plateful, for only the mistress and the master were allowed seconds, but she knew he must still be hungry. John and Acts could eat more than Bo had, and he was a very big boy.

After supper, Mistress Weston announced, "Bo will sleep in the storeroom, Hannah, so I suppose you will need to sleep here in the kitchen."

Hannah tried to hide her delight. She already had been sleeping in the kitchen, but Mistress Weston didn't know that. Now she wouldn't have to try to be up before the mistress caught her. She hoped Bo wouldn't be too uncomfortable in the dark, dusty storeroom, but she doubted that he was used to anything better, poor fellow.

She wondered if he could talk. He hadn't said a word since Master Weston had brought him into the tavern. Most of the time, he wouldn't even raise his eyes. He just stared at the floor, nodding or shaking his head if he had to answer some question of the master or the mistress.

After the Westons had gone upstairs to bed, Hannah took two leftover biscuits, tucked a piece of ham between each one, and carried them back to the storeroom. "Bo?" she whispered into the dark. "Bo, are you there?"

She felt his presence in the doorway, more than saw him. He was as black as the night around him, except for the whites of his eyes and the teeth he showed in a pleased grin when she handed him the biscuits.

"Bo beholden to you, ma'am," he murmured gratefully.

"You can talk!" Hannah exclaimed, already happily planning conversations they might have in days to come. She had gone from no friends at all to two new friends in the same day!

"Bo can talk," he mumbled around a biscuit. "He just doan say no more'n he haf to. Safer that way."

Hannah giggled, then put both hands over her mouth. If the mistress knew she had found something to laugh about, she reckoned she would make her work all night, too!

"Good night, Bo," she whispered, turning and going back into the kitchen to lie down on her cover before the fireplace. She wondered if the mistress had given Bo any kind of cover, and if he was cold or afraid in that dark, stuffy room. It was hard to imagine anyone as big as Bo being afraid of anything, but some of the biggest men on Riceland Plantation had been afraid of "hants" and would never pass the graveyard at night.

When she got up the next morning and went to store her cover in the storeroom, Bo was already up and gone. After a few minutes, she heard him come in the back door, go into the big room, and dump an armload of logs beside the hearth. Then she heard him go back out.

Hannah took the biggest skillet down from its hook over the fireplace, sliced hog shoulder into it, and set it over the fire. She cut slices from a loaf of bread the mistress had baked yesterday and put them in the oven beside the fireplace to warm. She counted out eggs—three for the master, two for the mistress, two for Bo, and two for herself. Then she reached back into the basket and slipped out another one for Bo. But knowing that the mistress carefully counted the eggs each day, she put one of hers back.

When breakfast was ready and the Westons were eating theirs in the big room, Hannah gave Bo his plate. He looked at the three eggs, three pieces of bread, and two pieces of meat, then looked at Hannah's one of each. He shook his head, pointing to first his plate and then to hers.

"It's all right, Bo," she assured him in a low voice. "I just don't eat that much. That's why I'm such a scrawny thing, I reckon." She laughed, but he studied her seriously. Hannah had the feeling he didn't believe her. "Eat, Bo," she urged, "before the mistress comes in here and we both get in trouble."

Obediently, he began to eat. When he had finished every bite, he licked the plate. Apparently, he hadn't had enough to eat in a long time. Hannah was glad she had shared her rations with him.

Bo got up and went outside. He came back with a huge armload of logs and put them by the fireplace for her. Then he picked up both water buckets and went back out. In a few minutes, he was back with fresh water.

"You need Bo to do anything else, Miss Hannah?" he asked seriously.

"I don't think so, Bo," she answered with a smile.

"You need anything, you just tell Bo," he insisted, as he left the kitchen.

She heard him go back into the storeroom. *Could he possibly like it back in that dark hole?* she wondered. Or did he just assume that was where he should stay until the master called him?

About mid-morning, the master came in the front door, waving a newspaper in one hand. "We're in here!" he shouted. "Peg, come look! The man at the paper says this is our advertisement right here!"

The mistress took the paper and looked. "I reckon it is," she agreed doubtfully. "It has the picture of a lion on it."

Suddenly, Hannah realized that neither of them could read! Why, she could read! Mistress Annabelle had praised her for learning so quickly. It was hard to believe that she, a slave girl, could do something her owners couldn't do! Should she say anything?

She could almost hear Samson saying, "Slaves done be havin' to survive, anyways dey can, missy!" *Maybe it would be better to keep this special ability a secret,* she thought.

"Does it say we have the finest food west of the mountains?" the mistress asked.

"It's supposed to," Master Weston replied doubtfully. "How do I know, Peg?"

Hannah slipped over to where she could read the paper without them being aware of it. Bold print, under the picture of a roaring lion, announced that the Brass Lion tavern was now open for business on Wapping Street. "The best food west of the mountains! Comfortable accommodations! Fair prices! Hezekiah Weston, proprietor," it read.

Hezekiah? Hannah thought. *No wonder the mistress calls him Weston!*

"We'll have business tonight!" Mistress Weston crowed happily. And she led the way into the kitchen to begin preparations for the evening meal.

As the clock on the mantel struck 3 P.M., Mistress Weston surveyed their handiwork with a smile of satisfaction. "I'm going upstairs to rest my eyes a bit," she said. "You keep a close eye on those bread loaves and don't let them burn!" she ordered.

Hannah sighed. There would be no stolen moments of freedom for her today, but the memory of her last escape and its consequences was still fresh. She wasn't sure she wanted to risk Mistress Weston's anger again so soon.

The mistress, though, came back downstairs after her

nap in a good humor, confident that customers would soon be arriving.

Before the sun had set, her predictions were fulfilled when four men came in and sat down in the big room, "the public room," the mistress called it. The master went to make them welcome, then sat talking with them for a while, as Hannah and the mistress scurried around taking and filling their orders.

Hannah was almost sorry to see the master lock the door behind them when the evening was over, for the Brass Lion had been a jolly place while they were there.

Chapter Eight

By Friday night, the public room was full, with nine men and four women occupying the tables, talking and laughing, eating and drinking, and keeping the mistress, Hannah, and even Bo busy fetching and carrying.

By the time the evening was over, Hannah had changed her mind about the tavern being a jolly place. She was so tired, she wished she'd never heard of a tavern! And then three boatmen decided to spend the night.

The next morning, after breakfast was over and their guests had gone out, Bo was set to scrubbing the mud from the floor of the tavern's big room, and Hannah was sent upstairs to put the dormitory in order.

As she straightened the covers on the beds and plumped the pillows, she could hear the mistress' voice downstairs, rising and falling in a constant complaint like endless rain on the roof.

Hannah emptied the dirty water from the basin into the chamber pot and carried it downstairs and outside. She had replaced it in the bedroom and was nearly back downstairs when she heard the slap of an open palm against bare flesh.

"You thieving lout!" the mistress cried. "Steal food from my kitchen, will you!"

Bo answered nothing, and Hannah heard another hard slap, then another. She put one hand up to her face, remembering.

"There'll be no food for you the rest of this day!" the mistress screeched. "Maybe then you will appreciate the good situation you've got here!"

Hannah stifled a bitter laugh. Bo's pallet in the back of an airless storeroom and a few leftover crusts and morsels didn't seem to her like a "good situation!" And her own lot was hardly better.

She could hear the mistress' footsteps heading for the kitchen, and she turned quickly to stir the fire and hang a fresh kettle of water over it.

"Weston will deal with you when he comes back!" the mistress threatened over her shoulder as she came into the room.

Poor Bo! she thought as she measured beans into the soup pot and added a ham bone for flavor, as Ma always had done. Bo really wanted to please, but he was just awkward and slow, and sometimes he didn't understand what his owners wanted of him.

Well, she thought, *until Bo came, I was the one always in trouble!* And while she felt sorry for Bo, she couldn't help but be relieved that she had not been the one receiving those slaps today. The mistress' big, rough hands could deliver quite a blow!

"Stir up a big batch of cornbread," the mistress ordered. "It's Saturday, and this place likely will be full of customers before dark!"

"Yes, ma'am," Hannah answered, picking up a heavy crock and heading for the storeroom to get the cornmeal. When she came back into the room, the mistress handed her two cold biscuits left from breakfast.

"We've got no time to fix a noon meal," she explained, "and with Weston out scouring the countryside for supplies, we won't have to worry about feeding him. Maybe he will shoot a deer," she added, as she spread butter and jelly on her biscuit without offering any to Hannah. "If trade keeps up like it's started, we could use some venison."

Hannah gnawed at a biscuit, casting an unhappy glance toward the door to the big room. She knew Bo was in there, tired and hungry. Did she dare to share a biscuit with him?

The mistress looked up and seemed to read Hannah's thoughts. She scowled. "You won't be giving any food to that lazy lout in there," she warned. "I caught him with a stolen biscuit and piece of ham from last night's supper. It fell out of his shirt as he bent over to scrub the floor."

Words of defense rose in Hannah's throat, but she swallowed them. She was sure the food was part of what she had taken to him again last night. Bo was being blamed for something she had done! But if she told the mistress she had been smuggling food to Bo, she would get the next beating.

"No, ma'am," she murmured, biting off a piece of the dry, hard bread. But the more she chewed it, the bigger it seemed to get, all wrapped up in a chunk of guilt that made it almost impossible to swallow.

Their meager meal finished, the mistress led Hannah in a feverish preparation of food for the evening. Hannah found herself longing for the hands of the clock to reach 3:00, the time the mistress usually went upstairs for her nap.

As the clock struck, Hannah took inventory. The beans were cooking and the cornbread was baking. Loaves of crusty bread sat on the table, wrapped in cloths. There was plenty of ham left for slicing, and eggs were handy for frying if someone ordered them. It was too early to make biscuits or coffee. Surely the mistress would take a rest today, and she could escape to the yard next door for a few minutes!

The mistress reached for her dough tray and rolling pin. "There'll be no time for rest this afternoon, I'm afraid," she sighed. "I've got pies to bake. Those men eat like they're half starved! I reckon it's been a while since they had some good home cooking. A piece of apple pie and a cup of coffee should fetch a pretty farthing this night, or I miss my guess!"

Hannah had to admit that the mistress had a fine hand with pastries, and her coffee never went begging for drinkers. Then she sighed. Another day would pass without a visit to Mrs. Crenshaw's or the grave by the river. It was likely that by the time she got back over there, the nice lady would have forgotten all about her offer of tea and conversation.

She sighed again, dumping the thick yellow cornmeal batter into the biggest iron skillet. She placed it carefully over the fire on its little legs and put the top on it.

Hannah heard Bo go out back to empty his scrub bucket. Then he came into the kitchen and grabbed two water buckets. She looked up with a smile of sympathy, but he kept his head down and his gaze on the floor as he carried the buckets out of the room. In a few minutes, he was back with fresh water. Then he brought in an armload of wood. Each time he came or went, Hannah repeated her smile, but he wouldn't look at her.

"Mercy, me!" Mistress Weston breathed. "There's the first of the crowd at the door already! Hannah, fill this coffeepot with water and set it on the fire. I'll finish making the coffee after I've let them in and taken their orders."

Before the night was over, Hannah had poured dozens of cups of coffee and served nearly all of four large apple pies. Finally, the last man had gone, except the three who were spending another night upstairs before they took their boat on downriver in the morning.

When the doors were locked and the master and mistress had followed the men upstairs, Hannah sank down on her pallet before the fire. She was so tired she thought her bones would sink right through the floor into the dirt beneath.

Suddenly, she remembered that Bo hadn't had anything to eat since breakfast, but at least the master had not "dealt with him," as the mistress had promised. Hannah supposed that in the flurry of waiting on their customers, she had forgotten about it, or had just been too tired at the end of this long day to care.

Wearily, she got up, dipped up a bowl of beans and laid a large piece of cornbread across the top of the bowl. As she turned to go, her glance fell on the remaining half of an apple pie. She hesitated, knowing Mistress Weston surely knew how much had been left in the pan. Defiantly, she cut the pie in half and placed one piece on a saucer. She poured a mug of milk, and juggling the three items, carried them back to the storeroom.

All she could see in the depths of its blackness were the whites of Bo's dark eyes and the flash of his teeth as he grinned up at her from his pallet on the floor.

"Thank you, missy Hannah," he whispered. "Bo beholden' to you!"

Again, guilt stung Hannah. She had contributed to his punishment today, and if the mistress found out she had fed him tonight, they both would be beaten.

"Don't try to save any of it, Bo," she cautioned. "I'll see that you get more tomorrow."

"Yes'um," he whispered. "Thank you, missy."

"Good night, Bo," she whispered back. "I'll get the dishes and wash them before she comes down in the morning."

The next morning, though, she awoke to the sound of heavy footsteps on the stairs. She had overslept! She jumped up, folded her pallet, and threw it behind the cupboard in the corner. There was no chance of getting Bo's dirty dishes back to the kitchen now without being seen.

She had just stirred the fire and was putting a fresh log on it when Mistress Weston came into the room.

"Get a move on, girl!" she ordered. "We've got three extra men to feed this morning before they leave, and I want them to carry word of our good vittles with them!"

As she worked side by side with the mistress, preparing the Sunday morning meal, Hannah tried to anticipate every need from the storeroom so Bo's empty dishes would not be discovered.

The three men ate their breakfasts with Master Weston, then left to continue their journey down the river. The master called to Bo to carry their luggage, and walked with them to the boat.

As Hannah gathered their dirty dishes, she heard the mistress cry out. Hannah's heart sank. She knew what she had found.

"That thieving lout has done it again!" She stormed out of the storeroom with the dishes in her hands. "And he had the nerve to dirty up my dishes this time!"

Hannah swallowed the fear that gathered in her throat. She couldn't let Bo take the punishment alone this time, she thought, as she heard the master come in the back door.

"Weston!" the mistress yelled. "I want that stupid boy beat

within an inch of his life! I sent him to bed without supper to punish him, and look what he's done!" She waved the dishes in her husband's face.

Hannah moved to the doorway. "I took the food, mistress," she confessed.

Mistress Weston whirled around. "You?" Her eyes narrowed to slits of anger. "I might have known! Weston, I want her whipped first, then. It appears she's the thief this time, but he joined right in and ate what she stole."

The master went to the storeroom doorway and reached around it for the leather strap. "Turn around, girl," he ordered.

Hannah shut her eyes, swallowed hard, and turned her back to him. She flinched as the first blow fell, and tears stung her eyes. As the next blow fell, she jerked sideways and felt the strap cut into her cheek.

She felt him raise the strap again and heard the whoosh as it came down through the air, but there was no blow.

"No more!" Bo yelled.

She heard the master curse and opened her eyes. Bo was standing over the master, his big fist clutching the strap above their heads, keeping it away from her.

"Why, you ornery, no-good rascal!" Master Weston panted, struggling to regain control of the strap. But Bo held on.

"No more!" he repeated, and Hannah saw a fire in his eyes she never had seen before. He didn't look dull now. He looked dangerous. If he hadn't been her friend, she would have been afraid of him.

The master hesitated, then jerked the strap free of Bo's fist. He glared at him, then turned and hung the strap back on its nail. "Get out there and cut some firewood!" he ordered, "and I want no more trouble from you!"

So far as Hannah knew, the master did nothing more to Bo that day, except keep him hard at chores. When he had done everything the master could find for him to do around the tavern and the stables, he set him to digging up a garden space just beyond the back door.

Hannah had little time to worry about Bo, though, or the way her back stung and her jaw ached, for even though it was Sunday and they usually ate a cold supper of leftovers from the noon meal, the mistress had her hard at work most of the afternoon.

"I look for a brisk trade even on Sunday, but I think we've got enough food here to feed an army!" Mistress Weston said finally, surveying the table and the fireplace. "I'm going upstairs to lie down before the rush begins. The coffee's ready to boil. Make sure you put the pot on the fire by five o'clock."

"Yes, ma'am," Hannah replied, thinking eagerly of slipping away next door. If she got caught, so what? It seemed that her life was going to be made up of beatings, anyway. She might as well do all she could to enjoy the brief moments in between.

She wouldn't bother Mrs. Crenshaw, she decided as she slipped through the hedge and headed down toward the grave. She didn't want her to ask questions about her torn face. She knew any interference from her would only make it worse for her and Bo. The Westons wouldn't take kindly to anyone meddling in their business.

There was a fresh bouquet of some pretty little pink flowers in a crystal vase on Miriam Elizabeth's grave.

Poor Mrs. Crenshaw! How lonely she must be, living in that big house all by herself! she thought.

Hannah sank down beside the grave and leaned her head back against the stone. She surely could sympathize with Mrs. Crenshaw.

"If anybody knows what it means to be lonely, Miriam Elizabeth, I reckon it's me!" she whispered to the little dead girl who might have been her friend. She wished the little girl were here, or that she could just lie down here on this quiet grave overlooking the river, go to sleep, and never wake up again. Certainly there was no one around here who cared if she lived or died, except maybe Bo, and he, like a mangy old dog, loved her because she fed him.

Of course, the mistress wanted all the work she could get out of her, but if she were gone, she knew the Westons would just buy another girl to slave for them. They didn't care who it was, as long as their work got done.

The sting of salt in the cut on her face made her aware that she was crying. Then, unable to stop the tears, she threw herself across the grave, sobbing aloud.

"There, there, child! What on earth is wrong?" Mrs. Crenshaw asked in alarm. She knelt beside Hannah and took her into her arms, rocking her back and forth, crooning comfort to her. Hannah's sobs increased.

Finally, the old lady eased her back against the stone, and Hannah saw her take a handkerchief out of her dress and reach out to dry her tears.

"Child, what has happened to your face?" she asked, pulling the handkerchief back in horror as she saw Hannah's cheek.

Hannah had stopped sobbing, except for a gulp now and then, but she couldn't speak. Her throat was still full of unshed tears.

Suddenly, Mrs. Crenshaw put her hand on the stone and pushed herself up from her knees. "It's those tavern keepers, isn't it?" she asked grimly. "They have done this to you!"

Hannah nodded.

"Wait here, child," she ordered. "I will have a word with them. If that is not sufficient . . ."

Hannah clutched at Mrs. Crenshaw's skirt. "Oh, please, don't say anything!" she begged. "If they think I have told you, they will beat me again!"

Mrs. Crenshaw studied her. Finally, she nodded. "All right, child. What did you say your name was?"

"Hannah," she answered. "Mrs. Crenshaw, please don't go over there! Please, if you really care, don't go!"

"Hannah, don't worry," the old woman said softly, patting her on top of her head. "I will not cause you more trouble. Your troubles will end here and now, for I am going over there to buy you from your owners."

Chapter Nine

Hannah followed Mrs. Crenshaw across the lawn and through the hedge. When she came into the back entry of the tavern, she heard voices coming from the big room, and tiptoed over to the doorway to listen.

"I am Rachel Crenshaw from next door," Mrs. Crenshaw was saying. "I would like to buy your girl, Hannah. Name your price!"

Hannah prayed the Westons would sell her! Surely working for Mrs. Crenshaw would be better than working for them! She didn't think Mrs. Crenshaw would beat her, for she had been horrified by the gash Master Weston had left across her cheek this morning. But her hopes died quickly, as she heard Mistress Weston's answer.

"Oh, we couldn't sell Hannah! I am training her to help me run this tavern, and she has proved to be a quick learner. I don't know how I would get along without her!"

Was the mistress talking about her? Hannah wondered. She had hardly given her a good word in all the weeks she had worked for them. More often than not, she had received a slap for her efforts.

Mrs. Crenshaw said something in a voice too low for Hannah to hear, and Mistress Weston answered, "Well, I'm sure a lady your age needs help, Mrs. . . . . Crenshaw, is it? But we're so busy with customers that I just don't have time to train someone new. And, of course, I've become very attached to Hannah."

Hannah almost choked on that. She eased around the door frame and found that, luckily, the mistress had her back to her.

"I wish you would reconsider, Mrs. Weston," Mrs. Crenshaw said. "I will pay you a price that is more than fair."

Somehow, Hannah knew that the mistress wasn't going to sell her, no matter what Mrs. Crenshaw offered. As greedy as she usually was, that was surprising.

"I have an idea that could benefit both of us," Mistress Weston said then. "We could hire Hannah out to you. I need her all day and evening on Friday and Saturday, but earlier in the week I probably could spare her some."

Hannah watched the expression on Mrs. Crenshaw's face, praying she would agree. She didn't care if she had to work twice as hard as she did now, if she could just get away from the Westons for a while each week.

"Of course, she helps with the washing on Mondays, but we could finish that early and I could spare her for about three hours or so that afternoon. Or I could let her go for about that long on Tuesday, Wednesday, or Thursday," the mistress went on. "Sunday, of course, is a light day, but I doubt that you'd want her then, anyway. Most people don't do their heavy work on Sundays," she added with her unpleasant laugh.

Mrs. Crenshaw glanced at Hannah, who pleaded with her silently. "All right, Mrs. Weston," she said crisply. "I will take her on Tuesday, Thursday, and Sunday afternoons from two until five o'clock, if that is satisfactory. Now, what will be your price?"

Hannah half listened as they discussed money, her head nearly spinning with delight at the prospect of getting away for a while three days a week. She didn't care what chores she would have to do!

"We will start immediately, then," she heard Mrs. Crenshaw say. She reached into the neck of her dress and pulled out a small purse on a chain. She fished out several coins and dropped them into Mistress Weston's waiting palm. "Come along, Hannah," she said, "you're going home with me for a while."

Hannah looked quickly at her mistress, but she was smiling as she counted the coins. Hannah followed Mrs. Crenshaw back outside, through the hedge, across the lawn, and into the tall brick house.

Inside, the house was cool and quiet, as Hannah waited for her eyes to adjust to the dimness.

"This way," Mrs. Crenshaw said, disappearing through a doorway. Hannah followed her across a hallway and into a square, tall-ceilinged room with a fireplace to her left at the back of the room. Sofas, chairs, and small tables were scattered over a thick, red-and-blue-flowered carpet that covered the middle of the floor, leaving two feet or so of golden wood showing all around it. The floor was in need of a good polishing.

"What do you want me to do first, Mrs. Crenshaw?" Hannah asked, eyeing the thick dust that lay like ashes over the dark wood of the mantel and the tables.

"First, you may call me Miss Rachel," she answered firmly. "'Mrs. Crenshaw' makes me feel old, which I am, but I don't like to be reminded of it so often," she said with a wry smile.

"Yes, Miss Rachel," Hannah said, grinning.

"That's better," the lady went on. "Now, you may come into the kitchen, and I will put some salve on that cut. Then, you may help me prepare our tea. We'll have it here at that little table by the window, where we can see the sunlight through the new leaves of the walnut trees."

"But ma'am, I thought I was here to work!" Hannah protested.

"Oh, you will work, dear," Miss Rachel assured her. "Next week, we will light into this dusty, musty old house and give it a thorough spring-cleaning like it hasn't had in years! I haven't had the heart to do much of anything since Miriam . . ." She stood lost in thought for a moment, then straightened her shoulders. "Next Tuesday will be soon enough," she said crisply, leading the way across the hallway and into the kitchen. "Right now, we are going to have tea."

"Yes, ma'am!" Hannah agreed, laughing, knowing she was going to love being with Miss Rachel, no matter how hard she had to work next Tuesday and in the days to follow.

The dainty cups and saucers Miss Rachel took from the

kitchen cupboard were covered with a pink design showing some lovely countryside.

"England," Miss Rachel explained when she saw Hannah staring at them. "My husband and I lived there for a time when we first were married. It was his home, and I grew to love it too. But the eldest brother inherited the Crenshaw estate, as is the custom there, and Allan, the youngest, decided to seek his fortune in America. He found it in the rich lands of Virginia." She stood staring at the cup in her hand, as if she had never seen it before.

"Why did you come to Kentucky, Miss Rachel?" Hannah asked, hoping her question would not be considered impertinent.

"Our only son was killed in the Revolution. His father was fighting alongside and saw him fall. After that, Allan wanted to get away from all reminders of that terrible day, so we came west. Soon after we settled here and built this house, Allan decided it was his duty to join in the Indian campaigns. He never came back. I was told he was dead," she said, placing the cups and saucers on a tray and adding silver spoons and white linen napkins.

"And you stayed here in this big house all by yourself?" Hannah questioned. "Weren't you lonely?"

"Well, dear, I had my little Miriam then." Absently, she picked up a sugar bowl and held it. "She was such a comfort to me, such a companion!" She set the bowl on the tray and added a small pitcher of cream. Then she picked up the tray and started back across the hall.

Not knowing what else to do, Hannah followed. "What happened to Miriam, Miss Rachel?"

"She took a fever. I nursed her day and night, but she just kept getting worse, just wasting away. Finally, there was nothing I could do to keep the Angel of Death from claiming her. There are no churches or synagogues within the city limits of Frankfort, so I buried her here in the yard, where I could tend her grave and keep fresh flowers on it."

"I am so sorry, Miss Rachel," Hannah said, her own troubles seeming small and unimportant in the face of such tragedy.

"Well, it has been a long time, Hannah," she said, wiping the dust from the table with her handkerchief and setting down the tray. "One learns to live with grief after a time. I survived the loss of my son on the battlefield, and my husband's death at the hands of the Indians, and went on because of Miriam. At her death, nothing else seemed to matter—not the wealth we had accumulated, not this house I had supervised so lovingly, not the faith I'd once had in the God of Jacob, Moses, and David. I just shut myself up in this big old mausoleum and waited to die."

"It's a beautiful house, Miss Rachel," Hannah said, looking around at the damask-covered sofas and the matching draperies at the tall windows, the velvet chairs and footstools, the rich dark wood of the tables and straight-backed chairs. "It reminds me of Gray Gables, the home of the people I belonged to in Charleston."

"How did you become the property of the Westons?" Miss Rachel asked. "Why did you leave Charleston?"

"My mistress and her baby died, and Master Alex had no further need of me," she explained. "He was selling the house and leaving Charleston, and the Westons were there looking for a slave to help with the tavern they planned to open in Kentucky. Master Alex said it was the best situation he could arrange for me on such short notice."

"Hummph!" Miss Rachel snorted. "It appears to me that the situation isn't such a good one for you, Hannah," she said, heading for the doorway. "Sit down, child," she ordered, seeing that Hannah was uncertain about whether or not to follow her. "I'll be right back."

Hannah perched on the edge of one of the chairs and began placing dishes from the tray on the table. She knew how to lay out a nice tea table. Lettie had taught her well.

What would Lettie think of all this dust? she wondered. Why, she would have been on her like a duck on a June bug if she had let dust accumulate as it had here in Miss Rachel's house! Tuesday, though, they would begin to put the house in order. Miss Rachel had said so. And there certainly was no mud and grime here like what she had had to clean at the tavern when they first came.

Miss Rachel came back into the room, carrying in her right hand a teapot that matched the cups, and in her left, a plate of tea biscuits. Hannah could see a thick line of jelly inside the biscuits. Mistress Weston never let her have jelly. In fact, it had been a long time since she had had anything sweet. Her mouth watered, as she jumped up to take the plate and set it on the table.

"I don't feel right with you waiting on me, Miss Rachel!" she protested. "I'm supposed to be waiting on you!"

"Never mind, child. You will wait on me until you're sick and tired of me, but today you are my guest for tea. Now, do you want one lump of sugar or two? And do you take cream in your tea?"

Hannah sank back into the chair. "Two lumps, please," she answered, with a sassy grin that contradicted her dignified voice. "And I don't take cream."

Miss Rachel passed the plate of biscuits. "Have all you want," she encouraged, and Hannah piled four on her plate.

Before the afternoon was over, she had told Miss Rachel all about her family and their life on Riceland Plantation, and was well into her time with the DuVanes at Gray Gables when the clock on the mantel struck five.

"I'm afraid it's time to go, Hannah," Miss Rachel reminded her. "I wish Mrs. Weston had agreed to sell you to me so you'd never have to go back there." She stood up and began to place their dishes on the tray. "Run along now before she changes her mind about letting you work for me. Tuesday afternoon will be here before you know it, and I will have a full schedule of work for us to do in our three hours."

"Good-bye, Miss Rachel, and thank you for my first invitation to tea. My sister, Esther, and I used to have tea parties with our rag dolls, but we never had real food!"

"You and your sister have Bible names, Hannah, names as Jewish as Rachel and Miriam. You will have to tell me about that the next time you are here. I'm Jewish, you know."

"No, ma'am, I didn't know," Hannah answered. She didn't know much about Jewish people. But if they were all as nice as Miss Rachel, it was no wonder God had made them His chosen people! "Good-bye!" she said again, heading for the door. "I'll see you on Tuesday!"

Hannah ran back to the tavern so she wouldn't be late and antagonize Mistress Weston on her first day with Miss Rachel. She could hardly wait for Tuesday to come, and she didn't want to do anything to make the mistress forbid her to work next door.

The mistress was in the kitchen preparing supper. "We have three unexpected guests, Hannah," she said. "Fix some eggs, while I finish slicing this ham and make some fresh coffee."

Hannah got down the heavy skillet and ran to the storeroom for eggs.

"I'll take them some of this bread to tide them over until supper's ready," the mistress said. Then she leaned close to Hannah and whispered, "After supper, I will be training you in some new duties."

Soon, the eggs and ham were on three plates and Hannah and the mistress had carried them into the public room. Mistress Weston took the coffeepot and refilled the men's mugs. Then she came back into the kitchen and sat down at the work table. She motioned for Hannah to join her.

"Come, sit down here at the table with me, and let me tell you what I expect of you," Mistress Weston said, a smug smile playing about her thin lips. When Hannah had taken the seat across from her, the mistress leaned toward her.

"These men are trappers who have just sold a winter's

worth of furs for a good price and will be breaking their journey here tonight," she said. "While they snore away the liquor
they're swilling down like pigs, I want you to relieve them of
some of the burden of such heavy purses. They will never know
you have slipped into the room, removed their purses from
under their pillows, lightened them, and put them back. Now,
mind you, don't take it all—just a little from each purse! They
may never realize some of their winter wages are gone, or if they
do discover it, they'll never know when or where it happened!"
She laughed delightedly, slapping her knee with one hand.

Hannah stared at her unbelievingly. All her life she had heard
the Gullah worship leaders teach the Ten Commandments:
"Thou shalt not lie. Thou shalt not steal. . . ." And her ma had rein-
forced the teachings with her own admonishments—even with
a switch for emphasis when the boys needed it. Never had
Hannah taken anything that did not belong to her! *Except for
the food I smuggled to Bo,* she remembered guiltily; but she
had paid for that—a heavy price of pain.

"Mistress Weston, please don't make me do this!" she
begged. "I will scrub the floors again, and polish all the furniture, and cook all night, if you need me to. Just please don't
make me do this wicked thing!"

The mistress' hand was quick and sharp across her cheek.
"How dare you call me wicked! I suppose your visit to the
fine house next door has made you uppity! But don't forget,
you belong to me, girl, and you will do as I say, without argu-
ment or judgment!"

What can I do? she wondered desperately. Could she run
next door and beg Miss Rachel to help her? But she knew
that would only result in her being forbidden to go there ever
again, and her afternoons of freedom would be gone almost
before they began.

She belonged to the Westons. Tonight, she had been
ordered to break one of the Ten Commandments, and there
was nothing she could do but obey.

Chapter Ten

Hannah's stomach rolled as she climbed the stairs to the room where the three men slept. Sweat beaded on her forehead and wet her palms. She wiped her hands down the sides of her skirt, then pushed the door open a crack and peered around it. In the faint light of a pale moon shining through the small window, she could see that the men all lay on their backs, their snores rising and falling in an off-beat rhythm.

She eased around the door, praying it wouldn't creak, and her stomach rolled again, as she smelled the odor of stale drink and soured breath. She half turned to leave, but the sting of salty sweat running down from her forehead into the cut on her cheek reminded her of the consequences of disobeying the mistress. Swallowing hard, she walked toward the first bed, her bare feet silent on the wooden floor.

Hannah slipped her hand beneath the pillow, her heart pounding so that she was sure it would awaken the man, but he continued to snore. She grasped the bulging purse in her hand, eased it from under the pillow, opened it, and took out four golden coins. She dropped the coins into her apron pocket. Then, remembering her mistress' greed, and reasoning that the coins would hardly be missed from such a store, she took out two more before she slipped the purse back under the pillow.

She let out a long, silent breath and turned to the next bed, then the next, taking exactly six coins from each purse. She refused to think about breaking the Ten Commandments or that she was now a common thief.

I am not a thief! she thought. *I belong to someone who is making me steal.* Somehow, there was a vast difference, and it eased her guilt feelings a little.

Suddenly, there was a snort and a grunt, and she heard the straw mattress crackle and the bed creak as one of the men turned over. Hannah froze with her hand on the door. What would happen to her if she were caught? Would the mistress help her? She knew, with certainty, she would not. She would blame it all on Hannah, and likely put on a good show for the men by screaming and yelling and slapping her around.

There was no further sound from the man, though. Apparently, he had just turned over in his sleep. Weak with relief, Hannah slipped out the door and down the stairs.

"See, you survived, girl!" Mistress Weston exclaimed as Hannah came into the kitchen where she was waiting. "How much did you get? Give it to me!"

Hannah fished the coins from her pocket and counted them into the mistress' outstretched hand.

"Eighteen!" the mistress crowed. "A good return for our efforts!"

My efforts, you mean! Hannah thought. *You did nothing!* But she knew better than to say it.

"This is more than we took in for food, drink, and lodging tonight! Girl, we have found a way to make this tavern pay!" the mistress exulted.

Hannah's heart sank. That meant she would be expected to repeat the chores of this awful night, probably every time they had lodgers. She would sink deeper and deeper into sin, and one night, when the bed creaked as a lodger rolled over, it would mean he was awake and had caught her with her hand in his purse. But what could she do? She belonged to Peg and Hezekiah Weston.

Suddenly, she wondered if the master knew of his wife's activities. Did he approve of this new way of making money? Or did he even care, so long as he had his jug? He seemed to spend more and more time with it these days, though he did enjoy talking with the customers.

Then Hannah wondered if the night's activity was new. Had the Westons supplemented their tavern income in Georgia by stealing from their guests? Was that the reason they had left Georgia in such a hurry to come to the wilds of Kentucky? Were they fugitives from the law, or from some victim seeking vengeance?

"I think this may be the biggest take we've ever had!" Mistress Weston crowed. "You're a natural, girl! You're gonna earn your keep, after all!"

It was the first time she had ever been praised by her mistress, but it gave her no pleasure. To please Mistress Weston, she had to displease God! Fear crawled over her. What would be her punishment from her Creator for breaking one of His commandments? The Gullah praise leaders had made it very clear what God had said about stealing.

"Well, it's bed for me!" Mistress Weston broke into her thoughts. "And you'd better do the same, girl."

Hannah heard her footsteps on the stairs, and got up to get her cover. The May nights were too warm to sleep by the dying embers of the fire they had to have to cook meals for the tavern. She spread her cover at the end of the room under the window and lay down, but sleep would not come. She kept reliving those awful moments upstairs.

The day had not been entirely bad, she reminded herself. There had been that lovely time at tea with Miss Rachel. If only . . . At last she fell asleep to dreams of belonging to kind Miss Rachel.

When she awoke, the ugliness of the night before came flooding back, but she pushed it away and tried to concentrate on getting breakfast for the men she had robbed.

The men came downstairs and went into the public room. She could hear them laughing and talking with the master as he poured them coffee. Hannah hoped she wouldn't have to serve them this morning, not after stealing from them last night! Maybe the mistress would do it.

Mistress Weston came into the kitchen, calling orders over her shoulder to Bo.

"Good morning, Hannah," she said cheerfully, helping herself to a thick slice of crisp bacon from the plate on the table. "Where's the coffee? Has Weston got it in there? I hope it's fit to drink!"

"Yes, ma'am," Hannah assured her. "I made it exactly like you do, and the biscuits are just like yours too."

"We'll see about that!" she answered doubtfully, taking one from the pan, breaking it open, and spreading it with butter and jelly. She bit into it and chewed slowly. Hannah was sure she would find something to dislike about it.

The mistress nodded. "Very well done, my girl!" she said, smiling her thin-lipped smile. "Almost as good as mine. Now, take some in to the men. I'll bring the butter and jelly and take their orders for breakfast."

Hannah wrapped the hem of her apron around her hand and picked up the hot bread pan. She was going to have to face the men, after all. She passed the bread, keeping her eyes on the pan, unable to look the men in the eyes. Even though they didn't know what she had done, she knew. She would be glad when they had gone, and she could try to put it all behind her—until next time. How long would it be before she had to go through that terrible ordeal again?

Soon after breakfast, the men left, each riding a horse and leading one that had carried animal pelts out of the wilderness and now carried back only a few supplies. She wondered if they would ever figure out that not only were their pack horses carrying lighter loads, so were their purses!

Hannah glanced at Mistress Weston to see if she, too, were thinking of their crime, but she had other things on her mind.

"We've got to get some chickens, Weston, and a cow," she said. "Buying from the farmers around here is costing us a fortune! There's plenty of room for a pen just beyond the stable, and surely some farmer will sell us a cow and some hens."

"You're right, Peg," he agreed. "I've already been dickering for a cow, and I think I know where I can get some chickens. Bo can start on a pen this morning, and tomorrow he can go with me to bring them back."

Hannah gathered the dirty dishes and began to wash them, but she could not get the terrible thing she had done out of her mind.

All morning she washed bedclothes and hung them to dry on the clothesline Bo had strung between two trees. Her thoughts were tormented by the shameful deed she had done last night, and the dread of having to do it again.

All afternoon, as she helped the mistress bake bread, she relived the terrible ordeal, and that night, she went to sleep with it on her mind. She awakened in the middle of the night in a sweat from a nightmare of being caught with her hand under a pillow. She prayed no one would ever again spend the night at the Brass Lion!

Then it was Tuesday, her day to work for Miss Rachel. She should have been eager for two o'clock to come, but today she dreaded it. How could she face Miss Rachel with such a crime on her heart? Maybe she could just pretend she had forgotten and not go today.

When the clock struck 2:00, though, the mistress surprisingly reminded her of their bargain. "Be sure to bring my money back with you!" she ordered as Hannah went out the door. "She only paid me for Sunday."

"Yes, ma'am," Hannah answered, suddenly eager to go, no matter how ashamed she was. *At least I will get away from this place and this woman for a while!* she thought.

"I'm in here, Hannah!" Miss Rachel called from the room where they had had tea on Sunday. "We'll start with the parlor," she said, as Hannah entered the room. "While you wash windows, I will clean the carpet. It's so big, I'm not going to try to drag it outside to beat it, but I will give it a good going over right here with a damp brush."

Hannah saw that most of the furniture had been pushed

back onto the bare floor, and Miss Rachel stood with a bucket in one hand and a brush in the other.

"First, though," she said, "come here and let me look you over. No more cuts or bruises?"

Hannah shook her head, avoiding Miss Rachel's piercing dark eyes. *There are no new cuts or bruises on my face or body,* she thought, *but my soul is scarred beyond healing.*

"All right, then," Miss Rachel said. "Take down the draperies and we will hang them outside for dusting and airing. That material just doesn't take to water." She held out the bucket. "Then you can wash the windows, inside and out, with this mixture of vinegar and water."

Hannah set about her assigned tasks silently. Miss Rachel, though, rattled on about various things, with Hannah responding only when she felt that an answer was required.

When their time was nearly up, Miss Rachel brought in a tray of tea and cookies and placed it on the little table where they had sat last Sunday. Hannah took a cup of tea and sipped it silently.

"Who are you, young lady?" Miss Rachel asked finally. "And what have you done with Hannah?"

"What do you mean, Miss Rachel?" Hannah asked, startled into looking up into the keen dark eyes. "I am Hannah."

"You aren't the same lively Hannah who had tea with me last Sunday, chatting about her family back on Sunrise Island and her position as lady's maid in Charleston," Miss Rachel said, shaking her head. "That Hannah certainly wouldn't sit here ignoring cookies, saying nothing!"

"I be sorry, Miss Rachel," she said listlessly, slipping back into her old Gullah speech without realizing it. "I . . . I just be havin' a lot on my mind." She longed to tell Miss Rachel all about the terrible sin she had been forced to commit, to ask her advice about how she might avoid doing it again. But she didn't want her new friend to know how low she had sunk since she was last here.

"Well, I liked that other Hannah better than this gloomy

girl helping me today, though she has worked very hard and made those grimy windows shine like they haven't in years! But I hope that other Hannah comes back soon."

Hannah picked up a cookie and nibbled at it without enthusiasm.

"You're Gullah, aren't you, Hannah?" Miss Rachel asked.

Hannah nodded, looking down at the uneaten cookie. "I'm sorry, Miss Rachel," she repeated. "I've been trying to talk proper English, but . . ."

"Oh, no, Hannah!" Miss Rachel protested. "I had a Gullah maid once. Her voice had the warmth of the sun and the freshness of the winds of the islands in it. You don't ever want to lose that, though of course it is good for you to learn to speak proper English, as I have learned. But you want to keep the beauty of your heritage from the islands, and even before that, from Africa. What do you remember of the islands with the most fondness, except for your family?"

Hannah closed her eyes and let memories of her life on Sunrise Island wash over her. "I remember the sun and the wind on my face, and the waves washing the sand from my bare feet as I walked along the beach," she said dreamily. "I remember swimming in the sea until the incoming tide would throw us onto the beach. I still can hear the sound of the sea and the sea birds, and I can smell the honeysuckle growing wild in the trees. I remember the freedom of being a child, even though I was a slave, and the joy of our worship at the Praise House. And I remember the pride of my family and other Gullahs in being the most skilled rice growers in America."

Miss Rachel nodded. "You see? It's those things you never want to let go, Hannah, that you want to pass down to your children, just as I was passing my treasures down to my little Miriam. I wanted her to know the rich heritage she had from the brave and battered Jewish nation that gave the world knowledge of the laws of God."

Hannah's mind went back to her earlier thoughts of how

she had broken God's law by stealing from the trappers last night. There would be no joy for her now, even in the Praise House on Sunrise Island. Her guilt would smother joy.

"But I also wanted her to know how all of us came from the lands of our birth and made our contributions to this new breed of people called 'Americans,'" Miss Rachel continued. "I wanted her to take pride in the fierce independence that inspired the glorious words of the Declaration we sent to the King of England and to all other despots who would enslave us—words like, 'We believe these truths to be self-evident: that all men are created equal; that they are endowed by their creator with certain unalienable rights; that among these are life, liberty, and the pursuit of happiness,'" she quoted. "Be an American to the very depths of your being, but take pride in the rich heritage that you, as a Gullah, are contributing to that brave new entity."

"Yes, ma'am," Hannah promised without conviction. *How can I be anything proud and brave when I have become a common thief?* she wondered. No matter how she tried to excuse it by blaming her mistress, she knew she was a thief!

Miss Rachel reached over and took Hannah's strong, dark hand in her thin, light one. "Hannah, what is it? You seem so sad today! Is there anything I can do to help you?"

Hannah studied the veined and wrinkled hand holding hers. How she longed to confide in its kind owner!

"Miss Rachel, I . . ." she began, just as the clock whirred and struck. Hannah looked up. It was five o'clock. "I have to go, Miss Rachel," she said instead, getting up from the table.

Miss Rachel sighed and let go of her hand. She handed her some coins. "Give these to Mrs. Weston, dear," she said. "I suppose I'll see you again on Thursday?"

Hannah nodded, took the money, and ran from the house, anxious not to antagonize her owner, but more eager to get away from Miss Rachel's probing dark eyes. In another moment, she would have told her everything.

Chapter Eleven

As the days slipped into June, Hannah was grateful that no travelers stopped at the Brass Lion, except one family headed west. They were so obviously poor that even the mistress had no interest in robbing them. "It ain't worth the risk," she said.

Hannah breathed a sigh of relief and went about her work humming under her breath.

Three days each week she went to Miss Rachel's. The elegant brick house gleamed with wax and polish now, and the sun shone through the sparkling windows.

Miss Rachel herself seemed different, walking about the house with her dark eyes sparkling like the crystal chandeliers and the brass door fittings. Even on days when Hannah could not come, she often saw her out weeding the long-neglected flower beds or pruning the "horse-sweat" hedges, that Miss Rachel said were English boxwoods. "I like the smell because I've always liked horses," she had said.

"I like the smell when I'm coming through them to your house," Hannah had told her, "but when I'm going back, it reminds me that my time here with you is over for two days!"

"I'm going to have to find a gardener," Miss Rachel commented one day, as Hannah came upon her weeding the rose garden. "I'm just too old and decrepit to prune and mow like it ought to be done. Anyway, I'd rather be arranging flowers for my lovely, clean house, or reading the Scriptures by Miriam's grave."

Hannah knew Miss Rachel did not believe in the New Testament that told about Jesus Christ. "Jewish people do not believe Jesus was the Messiah, whose coming we still await," she had explained one day when she offered Hannah the Old Testament to practice her reading. So she and Hannah had studied together from the history of the Hebrew people, Miss Rachel's ancestors, and they had read from the law and the prophets.

"You know, when we break one of the Ten Commandments, Hannah, we are guilty of breaking them all," Miss Rachel said, holding up a hand for her to help her up from her position on her knees by the rose bed. "Well, I have broken the most important one, the one that says we must love Yahweh—the One you call God—with all our hearts."

"Oh, Miss Rachel . . ." Hannah began, but Miss Rachel cut off her protest.

"No, child, it's true. I loved my Miriam more than anything, and I bitterly resented Yahweh for taking her from me."

She smiled at Hannah, patted her hand, and tucked it into the crook of her arm. "But now, when I visit that small grave, I treasure precious memories instead of holding onto grief," she said. "I don't really understand it, but somehow you have given me a new lease on life, child, and I am grateful for it. I just wish there was something I could do for you."

"Oh, Miss Rachel!" Hannah cried. "I live for my time here with you! I don't know how I could endure my life with the Westons if I didn't have these hours to look forward to!"

"I asked to buy you again. Did you know that, Hannah?" she said.

Hannah shook her head. "No, but I'm sure she refused. She'll never let me go, Miss Rachel. I'm sure of that."

"One never knows," Miss Rachel murmured. "It doesn't hurt to try. Now, come into the house and let me measure you for a new dress. Yours are getting a bit short, don't you think?"

Hannah looked down at the yellow dress her ma had made her to wear to her new job as the DuVane's maid in Charleston. It was faded now and mended in several places; and as well as being too short, it was tighter in some places than it should have been.

Suddenly, the memory of Mistress Weston snatching Mistress Annabelle's beautiful blue cloak came into her mind. She smiled. Mistress Weston couldn't take her new dress, for there would be no way it would stretch to fit her bulk. But would she let her have it? *Well,* she thought, *as Miss Rachel says, it won't hurt to try.*

Oh, how she wished the Westons would sell her to Miss Rachel! Here, though she often worked hard, she was treated almost like a child of the house, and not like a slave at all. Here she was invited to tea when the work was done, like regular folks, and she was treated with kindness and concern in every way.

"What colors would you like, dear?" Miss Rachel broke into her thoughts. "I think a nice, soft red would be pretty with your dark coloring, and maybe a pale green. What do you think?"

"Yes, ma'am," Hannah agreed. "I like both of those colors. I reckon yellow is my favorite, but this dress is about worn out."

"Well, I'll see what I can find," Miss Rachel promised, and Hannah went back to the tavern thinking of new finery to come.

"We're having overnight guests tonight," the mistress said, as Hannah came into the kitchen.

Hannah's heart sank. Would she be required to steal again tonight? She prayed the visitors would be poor, like their last guests, so Mistress Weston wouldn't bother robbing them! Then she saw the mistress' sly grin and knew what would be expected of her when the guests had gone to bed.

Knowing what she must do, Hannah could hardly look at the two well-dressed men who sat at the table in the public room, laughing and drinking with Master Weston. *How can the master treat them like old friends, knowing what will happen as soon as they are asleep?* she wondered. Or did he know? Maybe Hezekiah Weston had no idea what went on in his tavern after he had emptied his jug and gone to bed.

If she told the master, would he make the mistress stop? Or would he, too, slap her around for disobeying orders? She didn't know, and this was one time when Miss Rachel's, "It can't hurt to try," could be wrong! It could hurt very much if the master was a part of the mistress' plan and decided to enforce her obedience with his leather strap!

As she carried food and drink into the public room, Hannah noticed that one of the men had taken off his coat and laid a handgun on the table in front of him. She swallowed. It wasn't too hard to figure out what he would do if he caught someone trying to steal his money.

Later, butterflies began to dance wildly in Hannah's stomach when she heard the men climbing the stairs to the bedroom above. How long would it be before she had to rummage through their belongings to find their bulging purses?

The mistress came into the kitchen, carrying the last of the dirty cups. She smiled, a thin, hard smile that reminded Hannah of sly old Br'er Fox when he was thinking up mischief. And sure enough, her first words were, "Hannah, you know what to do as soon as they are asleep."

Hannah swallowed hard. Should she argue and get slapped around for it? Should she beg, with the same result? She knew none of her protests would do any good, but what else could she do? If she ran next door, they would come after her and punish her, and perhaps even take vengeance on dear Miss Rachel! If she ran away, they would surely find her. And the punishment for runaway slaves often was death!

"You do understand what I expect of you?" the mistress growled.

Hannah nodded, the butterflies settling in the pit of her stomach like cold grits. *All I can do is follow orders,* she thought, as she sat down at the table to wait for the men to fall asleep.

When darkness had settled over the tavern and she could hear the snores of the men upstairs, Hannah crept up the steps. She was too sick at heart to be afraid. She just placed one foot in front of the other and pulled herself up the stairs.

She padded silently down the hall and pushed against the

door, but it wouldn't open! Then she realized that the men had set something against it to keep intruders out of their room. Weak with relief, she turned to retreat, but Mistress Weston stood in her bedroom door, watching. She motioned angrily for her to go on into the room.

Hannah crept to where the mistress stood and whispered to her what the men had done. "I can't get the door open without waking them," she explained.

"You get in that room and do as I ordered!" the mistress hissed. "If you don't have gold for me before this night is over, I will have something for you in the morning!"

Hannah stared at her. The woman was mad! How could she get the door open without scraping whatever they had set in front of it over the bare wooden floor? At least one of the men was sure to hear her! Likely as not, he would shoot her!

"You will do as I say," Mistress Weston hissed again, "even if you have to climb in through the window! It's open."

Is she serious? Hannah wondered, studying the woman's narrowed eyes and the thin, hard line of her lips. She was!

"Get on with it!" Mistress Weston ordered, drawing back her hand in the threat of a slap.

Hannah backed away, then turned and went back down the stairs. She went out the back door and stood looking up at the wall of the cabin. The logs were chinked with a smooth line of mud and rock, crumbling in places, but not leaving enough space for a toehold between them.

She walked around to inspect the end wall, and her eyes lit on the jutting edges of rock that made up the chimney. She could probably find a toehold there, if the rocks weren't still hot from the supper fire. Gingerly, she touched one rock, then another. They were warm, but not hot enough to burn her.

Suddenly, she remembered the ladder Master Weston had used to clean the chimneys and repair the roof shingles when they first had come here. Relieved, she made her way to the stable. It was dark inside, even with the door standing open, but she felt her way along the stall rails and located the ladder against the back wall.

Their guests must have arrived by hired coach, she thought, for there were no strange horses in the stable. The master's horse gave a soft whinny as she dragged the rough, bark-covered ladder along, stirring up a musty flurry of dust and hay fragments.

Tugging the heavy ladder into place against the wall, she eased it up until it was propped against the eave. Quickly, she climbed the ladder, then crossed the sloping roof to the open window.

Again, the moon cast a pale light into the room, and she could see the men, one of them spread out on his back, and the other curled into a ball on his side. Both of them appeared to be sleeping soundly.

Hannah threw one leg over the windowsill, then the other, and dropped silently to the floor. She crouched under the window, waiting for the pounding of her heart to slow until she could hear the men's even breathing and know they still slept.

She edged across the bare wooden floor and around to the side of the first bed so that the man on his side had his back to her. Gingerly, she slipped her hand under the pillow, but there was nothing there! She eased to the other bed and again slipped her hand under the pillow. She recoiled as her fingers touched the cold metal of a gun.

She looked around the room. The men's valises sat beside the washstand that held the pitcher of water and its basin. Quickly, she searched the first valise, found the purse, and opened it. It wasn't as full as the purses of the three trappers she had robbed earlier, so she removed only a few coins and replaced the purse as she had found it. Then she did the same with the second man's valise and purse, placing the money in her apron pocket.

Crawling on her knees, she made her way back to the window, climbed over the sill, and back down the ladder. When she reached the ground, Hannah tugged the ladder away from the building and dragged it back to the stable.

Only after she was back inside the tavern, sitting at the kitchen table, did she allow herself the luxury of feeling. As she removed the coins from her pocket and spread them out on the table, she let the full force of guilt of what she had just done wash over her.

Too distraught to go to bed, Hannah laid her head down on the table, and finally slept there until daylight crept into the room. Stiff from the awkward position in which she had spent the latter hours of the night, she stretched her weary bones, rubbed the back of her neck, and went over to the fireplace to stir up the fire and put on the coffee.

"Good morning, Hannah!" Mistress Weston called cheerily as she came into the kitchen a little later. "Did you have a good evening?" She arched her eyebrows questioningly and spread her thin mouth in what Hannah figured she must think was a grin.

Knowing her mistress was not inquiring about her rest, Hannah held out the coins and dropped them into the mistress' outstretched palm.

"Only six?" the mistress grumbled. "Why didn't you get more? The men obviously were wealthy!"

"They carried less than the trappers, mistress, so I only took a few . . ." she began, but the mistress' slap cut off her words.

"You miserable wretch!" the woman said in a loud whisper, as the men's footsteps could be heard descending the stairs. "I'll take care of you later!" she promised, grabbing the coffeepot and disappearing into the hallway.

"Gentlemen, what would you like for breakfast?" Hannah heard her ask brightly as she entered the public room.

"I will not do it again!" Hannah vowed through clenched teeth. "I will not! No matter what she does!"

When breakfast was over and the men had gone, Hannah heard the mistress telling the master she wanted her beaten.

"What's she done now?" Master Weston asked, his voice betraying little interest in the matter.

"She has disobeyed my orders again," she said angrily, but

she didn't explain, so Hannah still wasn't sure the master knew what had gone on in the late night hours.

Suddenly, a cold determination came over Hannah. She threw down the wooden spoon she was holding and marched into the public room. The master sat at the table, holding a mug of coffee, with the mistress bending over him. She straightened when she saw Hannah, and her eyes narrowed.

"I will not steal for you again," Hannah said in a low, hard voice she had never used before.

"You what?" the woman screamed. "How dare you defy me! I will have you beaten within an inch of your life!"

"You can kill me, but I won't do it again!" Hannah said quietly, in that same hard voice.

"Weston! Did you hear this slave defy me to my face?" she sputtered furiously. "I want you to beat her! Now!"

The master rose wearily and went to get his strap. When he came back into the room, Hannah turned to face him.

"Master Weston, she has been forcing me to steal from the guests while they sleep," she told him. "I don't know if you approve of robbing your customers after they have paid to eat and sleep in your tavern, but I cannot do this anymore!"

"Peg, your thievery caused us to flee from Georgia with the law on our heels! Would you have the same thing happen here?" he grumbled, as he raised his arm to strike Hannah with the leather strap. Hannah flinched as the strap came down across her shoulders, once, twice, a third time.

Suddenly, there was a roar and Bo came charging into the room like a mad bull. He grabbed the strap away from Master Weston and struck him with it again and again. The master fell beneath the mighty blows, and still Bo kept hitting him.

The mistress picked up the poker from the fireplace and hit at Bo, but he whirled and struck her, too, knocking her to the floor. Then, throwing a tortured glance at Hannah, he threw down the strap and ran from the room. She heard the back door slam behind him.

Chapter Twelve

The master called in bloodhounds to search for Bo, but they found no trace of him. Hannah prayed they would never find him, for he was sure to be put to death now that he had beaten his master and mistress. And he had done it for her.

No overnight lodgers came to the tavern the rest of June or throughout July, so she was spared the testing of her resolve not to steal again. The mistress said no more about it, so she supposed the woman assumed she would do as she was told now, or maybe she was just waiting until the appropriate moment to reassert her orders.

Surprisingly, she still let Hannah serve Miss Rachel three afternoons each week, but of course, Hannah thought, she liked the money this brought into her greedy hands.

Miss Rachel was full of questions about Bo and why he had run away. Hannah told her the truth, up to the point of why she was being beaten when Bo stepped in to rescue her. She still could not bring herself to confess the terrible things she had done.

"Stand still, child! You're as fidgety as my Miriam used to be!" Miss Rachel said one afternoon, as she tried to fit the new red dress she was making for Hannah.

"Do you think Mistress Weston will let me keep the dresses?" Hannah asked wistfully.

"Surely she will be glad someone else is furnishing your clothes, as greedy as she is," Miss Rachel said. "And she certainly can't wear them, as she does the cloak she took from you!"

Hannah giggled. "She can barely get the cloak around her! But she wears it anyway."

"Well, there's no way she can get one of these dresses over that body," Miss Rachel insisted.

"She likes to punish me, though, Miss Rachel. She might take the dresses away just to be mean."

"She will not!" Miss Rachel said determinedly. "I will see to that! Now, stand still, child, before I stick you with this pin! I can't guarantee where it will go with you wiggling around so!"

"Yes, ma'am," Hannah said meekly, standing straight and holding her breath, as she watched Miss Rachel in the full-length mirror in front of her. Then she put up a hand to touch her hair. It was short and very curly again, since Miss Rachel had trimmed it.

"There!" Miss Rachel exclaimed, putting the last pin in place. "Now, take it off and lay it over there with the yellow one. I will have them ready for you when you come back again."

"Miss Rachel, we haven't accomplished anything this afternoon," Hannah said, feeling guilty that her friend was paying Mistress Weston and getting nothing for her money. "And now it's nearly five o'clock!"

"Then, we'd better hurry and have tea!" Miss Rachel said. "But, much as I love it, I think it's too hot for tea this August afternoon, so I have fixed us some lemonade. You get your old clothes on, and I will get the tray."

If only I could belong to Miss Rachel! Hannah thought wistfully, as she folded the red dress and laid it over the new yellow one across the back of the chair. She slipped the old yellow dress over her head and pulled it down over her hips.

"Come, Hannah, and let's have our lemonade and cookies," Miss Rachel urged. "We've only got fifteen minutes!"

Hannah took the tray from Miss Rachel and set it on the table. She pulled out a chair and seated her, then sat down across from her.

"I am going to raise my offer to Mrs. Weston," Miss Rachel said, passing a plate of iced sugar cookies. "I keep thinking that if I just offer her enough money, she will agree to sell you to me."

Hannah shook her head. "She won't, Miss Rachel. She knows how much I enjoy being here. She will never sell me to you!"

"Well, dear, as I always say, it never hurts to try."

Hannah heard the whir as the clock on the mantel prepared to strike. How fast the hours went here with Miss Rachel, and how they seemed to drag by on lead feet at the Brass Lion!

As she ran in the back door of the tavern, Hannah heard Mistress Weston say, "Of course, we have room for you to spend the night! If you don't mind sleeping in the same room, there's a bed for each of you."

Hannah's heart sank. The time had come for the testing of her vow not to steal again!

She heard the men laugh. "We've slept side by side on bedrolls on the trail, and four in a bed at the forts! I reckon a bed apiece, even in the same room, will be downright luxury!"

"Is that you, Hannah?" Mistress Weston called.

"Yes, ma'am," Hannah answered, coming to the door of the public room, where she saw three men dressed in buckskin sitting at a table. They each had one of the heavy tavern mugs in front of them, and one of them shuffled a deck of cards through his fingers.

"We have guests for the evening," the mistress said. "Let's see what a good meal we can set before them." She smiled her leering smile and arched her eyebrows at Hannah.

Hannah pretended not to see. "I'll start supper," she said, turning to go back into the kitchen.

Soon the mistress followed. "A rich night for us, my girl!" she crowed, picking up a knife and slicing into a crusty loaf of bread. "They carry the wealth of a settlement, on their way to buy supplies in Virginia. Of course, we won't take it all— just enough to help us and not hurt them too badly!"

Mistress Weston's unpleasant laugh crawled down Hannah's spine, but she went on frying ham in the big iron skillet over the fire, wiping the sweat from her face with the hem of her apron.

The mistress put the bread in the oven to warm and set a

fresh pot of coffee on the fire. "I'm so glad Weston brought us those chickens," she said. "Eggs cost us practically nothing now, except a little corn and some effort. I'll get some to go with that ham." Humming under her breath, she went to the storeroom.

It seemed to Hannah that they no sooner had taken the plates of food to the men than they were calling for more. But she hoped they would sit there eating, drinking, and playing cards all night. All too soon, though, she heard their footsteps mounting the stairs.

"You know what to do, girl," the mistress said, sticking her head in at the kitchen door on her way upstairs. "And I expect you to place more than six coins in my hand in the morning!"

"Mistress Weston," Hannah began, "please don't make me do this again! I will do anything you ask of me. Just don't make me do this!"

The mistress turned to stare at her, as though she couldn't believe what she had heard. Then her eyes narrowed. "You will do what I say, girl," she said between clenched teeth, "or I will see that Weston beats you within an inch of your life!"

Hannah swallowed hard. "Beat me, then, mistress, but don't make me do this!"

Suddenly the mistress smiled, a grim, thin-lipped smile. "All right, girl. You don't have to do it."

Hannah watched her warily. She supposed she should have been relieved, but she knew it wasn't going to be that easy.

"But your days next door with your precious Miss Rachel are over! Do you understand?" the mistress said with a mocking smile.

Hannah looked down at her feet, trying to hide her emotions. She knew that to let Mistress Weston know how badly her punishment hurt would only encourage more of the same.

"Yes, ma'am, I understand," she answered, meeting the woman's narrow gaze without flinching.

The mistress nodded, and apparently satisfied that she would be obeyed, went on upstairs.

Hannah sank down on the bench by the table and laid her head on her crossed forearms. She would have to wait until all were asleep before attempting to fulfill her assigned task.

"I can't do it!" she said aloud, raising her head. But how could she refuse? The promised beating was nothing compared to the threat that she could never go back to Miss Rachel's!

A loud snore from upstairs told her that at least one man was asleep. She glanced at the open window at the front of the kitchen. It was as black as the inside of a tunnel outside. Inside, the faint glow from the dying fire threw flickering shadows over the log walls. Out back, she could hear the lowing of the master's new cow, calling to the calf she had been forced to leave behind on the farm. But in here, except for the ticking of the clock on the public-room mantel and the snores upstairs, the tavern was wrapped in silence.

Were there more snores in the room above, now? She couldn't be sure all three men were asleep, but if she had to be a thief, she supposed she'd better be about it. She sighed and pushed herself up from the table.

As she placed one foot on the bottom riser of the stairs, the butterflies tumbled wildly in the pit of her stomach. Nausea rose in her throat. *How can I do this terrible thing again tonight and then face Miss Rachel the day after tomorrow?* she wondered. Yet, if she didn't obey the mistress, she knew she would never be with Miss Rachel again.

Either way, I lose Miss Rachel, she thought despairingly. *And she's the only good thing in my life!*

All at once, Hannah knew what she had to do. She turned from the stairs, went into the storeroom, and grabbed her other dress and the shawl Mistress Weston had given her in exchange for Mistress Annabelle's blue cloak. She carried them back into the kitchen, spread the shawl on the table, and rolled the dress up on top of it. Then she added a loaf of bread, a knife, and a tin mug.

She looked around, and her gaze fell on two leftover

sweet potatoes in a wooden bowl. Quickly, she wrapped them in a small cloth and added them to her pile. Then she tied two corners of the shawl together and repeated the process with the other two corners.

She ran back to the storeroom, got her shoes, and though they were getting too tight, stuffed her feet into the soft leather. Even feet toughened from going summer bare would need protection from the rough traveling she must do.

Then Hannah dug in a crack in the crumbling chinking between the logs, and pulled out the two gold coins Master Alex had given her that day on the wharf at Charleston when he had left her to the mercy of the Westons. She carried the coins back into the kitchen, held them in her hand a moment, then laid one on the table to pay for what she had taken. The other, she tucked into her bundle.

What would Master Alex do if he knew how she was treated by the people to whom he had sold her? But even if she could find him, she knew he could do nothing to help her. She belonged to the Westons, and there was nothing she could do but obey them.

Or run away! she thought, slipping the back-door latch carefully out of its holding bar and pushing the door open wide enough to squeeze through. She eased the door shut behind her and leaned against it.

There was no moon, and only a few stars had braved the dark sky. She could barely see her hand before her. It was just another shape of darkness, like the outline of the stable to her left. Beyond it, the stone house was visible as a lighter shadow among shadows.

To her right, Miss Rachel's brick house had disappeared into a shroud of trees and darkness. She wished she could say good-bye, could tell Miss Rachel how much their time together had meant to her. But the less her friend knew about her disappearance, the better it would be for Miss Rachel if the Westons came to question her.

The darkness was like a thick cover around her. Would she be able to make her way through it to put enough distance between her and this place before daybreak, when her disappearance was sure to be discovered? How long did she have? It was well into the early morning hours, for she had heard the clock strike midnight some time ago.

Where should she go? The master had set bloodhounds on Bo's trail. She felt sure he would do the same with her. She had heard talk on Sunrise Island of how runaway slaves would wade in streams to destroy any scent the hounds might have followed. Here, though, there was only the river. She was a strong swimmer, but how could she get her bundle across without getting it wet?

If she went down to the riverbank, would there be a boat she could use to cross the river? But if she left it on the other side, wouldn't the handlers simply bring the dogs across and start them on her trail there?

She edged around the corner of the tavern and walked toward the street in front of it. Maybe she should just follow the road out of Frankfort and wade the first stream she found, hoping it would be soon enough to escape the relentless hounds.

Hannah took a deep breath, entered the street, and turned to her right. She strode rapidly down the dirt track, hoping there were no bumps or holes to trip her in the dark.

Suddenly, the moon came out, impaling her dark figure in the middle of the road, exposing her to any who might be watching. She edged over toward the trees at the side of the road, praying no one had seen.

For a time, she stumbled along inside the line of trees, then moved over to follow along the top of the riverbank. From the tree-lined cliffs, a screech owl gave his lonely call, and was answered from somewhere upriver. She glanced quickly at the opposite bank, where the eerie green glow of phosphorous, or wildfire, winked at her from under rocks and fallen logs. Or was it all wildfire? Were the eyes of wild animals watching her too?

She shuddered. Then under her breath she began to sing some of the Gullah songs they had sung at the Praise House back on Sunrise Island. It pushed the fear away, and enabled her to keep up a steady progress away from Frankfort.

By the time the sky began to lighten, her empty stomach had been grumbling for some time. She sat down on the roots of a huge sycamore tree, opened her bundle, tore off a chunk of bread, and ate it hungrily. She wondered how far she had come. It seemed that she had been walking forever! But she knew she couldn't be far enough away from the tavern to rest long. Soon she was off again, heading upstream. She had no idea where she was going, but she knew she had to keep traveling or be caught. Often, runaway slaves did not get a second chance!

As the sun's rays touched the water, she heard the hounds. Fear drove her over the riverbank and into the water. She slung her bundle over her shoulder and waded out into the water. Soon she felt the bottom slip away from under her feet. She began a slow, one-handed side stroke that, with the steady movement of her legs and feet, propelled her out into the stream.

Suddenly, the current grabbed her, whirled her around, and pulled her under. She came up sputtering. Struggling against the unsuspected strength of the current, she swam toward the opposite shore. At last, her feet touched bottom again, and she waded onto the rocks.

She reached for her bundle, and found it still hanging from her shoulder, but it was thoroughly soaked. She supposed the bread, at least, was no longer edible.

Hannah looked up. The cliff rose steeply in front of her. To climb it would be extremely difficult, if not impossible. She listened intently. She had heard no baying of hounds behind her for some time now. Maybe they had given up and gone home.

Suddenly, the deep bay of a bloodhound traveled over the water, joined by the baying of other hounds. They were closer than they had been the last time she had heard them. Blindly, she plunged back into the river and waded frantically upstream.

Chapter Thirteen

Hannah awoke, stretched, and looked around, puzzled by the leafy roof above her and the sweet scent that tickled her nose. Then she remembered taking shelter from a light rain under the drooping branches of a giant cedar tree. She crawled out into the early morning sunlight, straightened her dress, and ran her fingers through her short curls.

"You might as well be quiet!" she told her growling stomach. She had thrown away the soggy bread the river had ruined, and she had eaten the two sweet potatoes long ago. Yesterday she had found some blackberries, but they too were gone now.

How long has it been since I left the tavern? she wondered. *Three days? Four?* She hadn't heard the hounds since the afternoon of that first terrifying day. She supposed they had given up when they lost her trail at the river.

Surely she had put many miles between her and Frankfort by now, but she couldn't be sure she was safe yet. Maybe she never would be. Maybe the Westons would pursue her until they finally caught her, no matter how long it might take.

She wished she could have seen Mistress Weston's face when she came into the kitchen that first morning and found her slave girl gone. She could imagine the screaming fit she had thrown, and the master would have responded by calling for the bloodhounds again. Or maybe one of them had gone next door first to question Miss Rachel. They might think she was hiding her, or that she had helped her run away.

What did Miss Rachel think about her leaving? Would she be disappointed in her, or would she understand why she had to go? But how could she understand, when she knew nothing

108

of the robberies Hannah had been forced to commit? Certainly Mistress Weston wasn't going to tell her!

Most importantly, would Miss Rachel miss her? Miss Rachel had seemed so much happier lately, arranging flowers to decorate her gleaming house, baking special treats to go with their tea, chatting merrily as they worked or rested. She had been a lonely, bitter old lady until Hannah had become her friend. But perhaps Miss Rachel would find a new girl to share her stories of the old days, to feed sugar cookies and lemonade, to give the dresses she had made for Hannah.

She felt tears gathering in her throat, and swallowed hard. *It's not the things Miss Rachel gave me that I miss so much,* she thought. *It's Miss Rachel herself!* But she had learned to live without her ma and without Mistress Annabelle. She would just have to learn to do without Miss Rachel too, she told herself firmly, pulling on her shoes.

She stood gingerly, wiggling her toes to more comfortable positions within the cramped space. The shoes seemed to have shrunk from their dousing in the streams she had waded. There was a split in the leather along her right big toe and a hole worn through beside her left little toe. Before long, she reckoned she would be barefooted.

She made her way to the edge of the trees and peered into the road. It was empty. Perhaps she could walk there a while. It was easier than stumbling over roots in the forest or stepping into groundhog and rabbit dens in the meadows. She had no idea where the road might lead, though the position of the sun told her she was heading somewhat south of east. She only knew she had to keep putting miles between her and the Brass Lion.

The sun was high overhead when she heard the rumble of wagon wheels behind her. A bend in the road hid whoever was back there from her sight. She dashed for the trees, but before she could reach them, a pair of brown mules came around the bend, pulling a wagon filled with black people.

"Whoa!" the driver called, pulling back on the reins.

"Whoa, Caleb! Whoa, Sophie!"

Hannah froze there by the side of the road. There was no use running now, for at least the driver had seen her.

"Hey, dere, young'un!" he called when he had the mules under control. "What you be doin' out here in de country all by yo'sef?"

"Don't yell, Rufus!" a woman scolded from back in the wagon. "It's jes a little girl. Come here, honey," she said, standing up and holding out her hand.

Hannah hesitated. Could they be sent by the Westons with a promise of a reward for bringing her back? But there were several children in the wagon. Surely this was just a family traveling somewhere, and no danger to her.

She walked over to the wagon and looked up into the soft dark eyes of a large black woman, nearly as large as Mistress Weston. In her arms she held a small child, and three others sat on the floor of the wagon bed.

"Where you be goin', honey?" the woman asked kindly.

"A runaway, mos' likely," the man grumbled.

Hannah studied the worn-looking little man with his shiny bald head framed by a curly fringe of gray hair. He seemed more curious about her than threatening.

"Yes, sir, I be a runaway," she answered truthfully, slipping back into Gullah speech without realizing it. "Will you be turnin' me in?"

The man's dark eyes twinkled under thick gray brows. "Now, why would I be doin' that, young'un?" he asked. "Seein' as how we be de same color and talk de same language. Likely we come from de same situation."

"Rufus! We're not runaways!" the woman protested. "We be free blacks, honey," she explained to Hannah. "Freed by our master out of the kindness of his heart, though we still plan to live and work on his place. But right now, we be travelin' to the great preachin' at Cane Ridge. You come along with us," she invited, motioning toward the wagon bed. "There be plenty of room."

"Jamaica!" the old man said. "Jes' cause I won't be turnin'

her in don't mean I be heping her run away! Do you know what'll happen to us if we be caught harborin' a runaway? And de ink hardly dry on our free papers!"

"What's one more black young'un in a wagonload, Rufus?" the woman answered. "Who would be knowin' dat dis 'un not be one of ours?"

"The folks she be belongin' to, that's who!" He turned to Hannah. "Where you be from, chile, and what be yo' name?"

"Do you be Gullah?" Hannah asked. The old man certainly sounded like it, but she wasn't sure about the woman. Her voice had a musical lilt and a slurring that was like the Gullahs of the Atlantic Sea Islands, yet there was something different about it.

"I be Gullah, from St. Helena Island," the man admitted. "Jamaica's fambly be from de West Indies, but she be raised on St. Helena, like me."

"My ma be from Jamaica," the woman explained. "I bein' her firstborn, and she bein' homesick, she named me for her old home in the islands of the Caribbean Sea."

"I be Gullah, too," Hannah said excitedly. "I was born on Riceland Plantation on Sunrise Island."

Rufus nodded as though he knew Sunrise Island. "How come you be so far from home, young'un?"

"My name be Hannah," she answered his earlier question. "I be sold to a family in Charleston," she continued, "then, when my mistress died, I be sold again. This time, my mistress be the meanest woman on the face of the earth! I had to run away!" She didn't want to go into the reasons.

"Our master left the islands after his wife and two of his little ones die of the fever. The mosquitoes be terrible bad on St. Helena," Rufus said gravely.

Hannah nodded. Master Benson paid little mind to the mosquitoes, but she knew that many plantation owners would not stay in the islands in the summer because of them, and would leave their plantations in the hands of their black overseers until the mosquitoes left in the fall.

"Dis week, our master go to de great revival at Cane Ridge Meeting House. Den, he come home and set all us slaves free, on condition we go to de revival ourselves. I doan know 'bout de others, but we be on our way!" Jamaica added, with a toss of her turbaned head that made her gold earrings swing. "Come with us!" she invited again.

Hannah glanced at Rufus. He studied her seriously, then grinned, exposing one gold tooth. "Climb in," he said.

Hannah climbed up over the wheel into the wagon bed, and Rufus clucked to the mules and slapped the reins lightly against their backs. The mules flicked their ears and started up the road at a leisurely pace, as though the whole thing was their idea.

Hannah took a seat between two giggling little girls with their hair tied in little pigtails. They grinned up at her.

"We be goin' to the 'vival," one of them offered.

"It be a big thing in dese parts!" the other one added.

Jamaica shifted the sleeping baby from one arm to the other. "Our master, I mean our former master, say dere be upwards of 20,000 people inside the Cane Ridge church and scattered over de grounds, listening to five or six preachers at a time."

"You ever been in a Praise House?" Hannah asked wistfully.

"I reckon so!" Rufus exclaimed. "I be linin' out de songs for many a meetin'!"

Jamaica nodded. "Can't nobody line songs like Rufus," she said.

The two little girls began to clap their hands in rhythm, and the whole family began to sing. Recognizing the song, Hannah joined in, grinning at the little boy about Romy's size sitting alone at the back of the wagon.

When that song and another one had been sung, Rufus cast an eye at the sun overhead. "'Pears to me it be about noontime," he said. "Jamaica, hand out some bread and meat and we be eatin' while we travel. I want to get to the meetin' early so we can be gettin' a place."

At the mention of food, Hannah's empty stomach growled loud enough for all of them to hear.

Jamaica looked at her questioningly. "Honey, when did you last be havin' somethin' to eat?"

"I don't know," Hannah answered. "I finished my rations a couple of days ago, but I had some berries yesterday."

"Oh, chile, I be so sorry! And us with dis basket of food jes settin' here!" She reached into the basket and handed her a thick slice of cornbread and a piece of boiled pork.

Hannah grabbed the food and crammed some of the bread into her mouth. "I be thankin' you," she said around it, chewing and swallowing, then stuffing another chunk into her mouth.

"Whoa, there, chile!" Rufus cautioned. "Slow down! You be makin' yo'sef sick."

She nodded, swallowing again. She raised the meat to her lips, but suddenly her stomach rolled and nausea rose in her throat.

Jamaica reached out and took the meat from her. "You been without too long, honey. Eat the bread first, chew slowly, and wash it down with some of this water," she said, handing her a jar.

Hannah chewed and swallowed, then took a sip of water. It was lukewarm, but it washed the dry bread down nicely.

She looked up, straight into the solemn eyes of the little boy in the back. She offered him the jar of water. "I be Hannah. What be your name?" she asked, again thinking of Romy.

The little boy ducked his head, then rolled his big, dark eyes up to look at her shyly.

Jamaica chuckled. "Dat be Luther," she answered for him. "He be three, but he doan talk much yet."

Hannah smiled at him. "You remind me of my little brother, Romans," she said. "I be missin' him very much."

Luther looked down at his food. Then he turned his back on all of them and finished eating, riding backward.

The little girls giggled and whispered to each other, looking at Luther.

"Girls! Don't be teasin' your brother," Jamaica scolded.

"Yes'um," they said in unison. They went back to eating, not looking at each other, trying their best not to giggle.

Hannah felt a great homesickness come over her for her own family back on Riceland Plantation, but she pushed it away. There was no way she could be with the people she loved, not even Miss Rachel. *Oh, well,* she thought, *I've got a way to travel, and I've got food in my stomach.*

After the basket of food was packed away, Jamaica and the children dozed as the wagon jolted along. Hannah suspected Rufus dozed a little too, letting the surefooted mules pick their way along the dirt road.

I could walk faster than this wagon travels, she thought, putting her bundle behind her to cushion her back against the wagon, *but ridin' sure be easier on my achin' feet!* She slipped off her shoes and wiggled her toes. Then she leaned back and closed her eyes.

Hannah was dreaming of bees droning in the honeysuckle outside the Praise House, but when she opened her eyes, she saw that the wagon had stopped, and it was not the drone of bees she had heard, but the sound of people's voices, thousands of them! As far as she could see, camps had been set up—under wagons, under trees, under makeshift tents in the fields. People even had staked their claims to spaces between the graves of a small cemetery beside the log church.

When Rufus finally found them a place to park out in the woods under the branches of a giant oak tree, Hannah helped them set up camp, then took her bundle and walked back toward the graveyard.

Making her way through the people camped there, Hannah walked among the tombstones, some of them nearly as tall as she was, reading the names and the dates of birth and death inscribed on them. Then she wandered among the graves marked only by rough rocks stood on end, wondering about the lives and deaths of the unknown people buried beneath them.

Finally, she sat down with her back against a tall stone, much as she had done that day in the backyard of the tall brick house, when her visit to little Miriam's grave had ended in her making friends with Miss Rachel. Maybe this graveyard would bring her good luck too.

Or had it been luck that brought her Miss Rachel, just when she felt she couldn't endure belonging to the Westons another day? Had God truly been looking out for her, as Ma had promised He would? But she had broken one of the Ten Commandments since then. God surely was through with her now!

Not even Miss Rachel would have anything to do with me if she knew, she thought sadly. They had read the Ten Commandments together, and Miss Rachel had said, "To break one of the commandments is to be guilty of breaking them all!"

What is Miss Rachel doing right now? she wondered. From the position of the sun on the western horizon, she reckoned it was about tea time. Had she found somebody to share it with her?

"It doan matter," she murmured aloud. Then she corrected herself: "It doesn't matter." It had been so easy to slip back into the soft Gullah speech, but she couldn't let herself forget the proper English Mistress Annabelle had worked so hard to teach her. It could be important in any new position she might find.

What am I going to do? she wondered suddenly. She had been so intent on getting away from the Westons, she had not thought much about the future. But once her visit to Cane Ridge was over, she'd have to find a way to make a living.

Maybe she could hire out to Rufus' and Jamaica's former owner. Surely not all of his freed slaves had stayed to work for him, as Rufus and Jamaica had, and he would need extra help.

Or maybe she could hire out as a lady's maid. She had learned a lot about that from Lettie and Mistress Annabelle, as well as from Miss Rachel. Or maybe she could be a cook. She had learned about that from both her ma and from Mistress Weston, for she had to admit that in spite of her many faults, the mistress had been a good cook. Or maybe . . .

Hannah yawned and slumped down against the stone. A breeze stirred the hot August air, and the drone of voices washed over her like waves over the sand on Sunrise Island.

Chapter Fourteen

Hannah sat up and looked around. The sun was a fireball on the western horizon, casting a strange light over the graveyard where she lay, and there was singing all around her. Hannah felt a chill slide down her spine. Had she died in her sleep? Were those angel voices she heard singing praises to God?

Then she realized the singing was coming from inside the log church beside the graveyard. People around her took up the song, and it spread through the grounds and into the woods.

When the song had ended, a voice cried from inside the church, "For all have sinned, and come short of the glory of God!" A low moan went up from the crowd in the church, spread through the churchyard, and was taken up by the thousands scattered over the fields and forest. Hannah wondered if they knew why they were moaning. Surely they couldn't hear the preacher way out there!

"Romans 3:23 tells us that," the voice continued. "As Jonathan Edwards proclaimed, 'We are sinners in the hands of an angry God,' and all our creeds and catechisms will not keep us from the fires of hell!"

Hannah felt the condemning words cut straight to her heart. She knew she was a sinner! Her soul was scarred with the stealing she had done for Mistress Weston, and she was sure she had done other things displeasing to her Maker. She found herself moaning softly with the rest.

"But there is hope, brothers and sisters!" the voice shouted. "Isaiah 53:6 tells us, 'All we like sheep have gone astray; we have turned every one to his own way; and the Lord hath laid on Him the iniquity of us all!' Or as John 3:16 puts it, 'For

God so loved the world, that He gave His only begotten Son, that whosoever believeth in Him should not perish, but have everlasting life!'"

A cheer went up from the crowd and echoed through the hills and valleys.

"*Whosoever,* brothers and sisters!" the voice cried. "That means you and it means me. Confess your sins! Ask for forgiveness! Put your faith in the sacrificial death of Jesus Christ, the Son of the Living God, and ye shall be saved!"

The crowd surged around Hannah, some shouting "Hallelujah," some sobbing, some calling out for mercy. A man beside her fell to the ground and lay there as though he were dead. A woman began to laugh uncontrollably.

Men that she assumed were preachers moved through the crowd, stopping to pray with one, or to rejoice with another. She saw one climb up on a stump out in the field and another mount a wagon and begin to preach to those too far from the church to hear the preacher inside.

Is that all there is to it? Hannah wondered. How good it would feel to be rid of her guilt! But how did she go about it? She had been happy in the services of her childhood in the Gullah Praise House, but she really did not know much about God.

"This revival is not about denominations or traditional 'religion,' brothers and sisters," the first preacher shouted above the noise. "I am a Presbyterian. My brother over here is a Methodist. That one over there is a Baptist. This revival simply is about a relationship with the Creator through the reconciliation bought by the blood of His Son, Jesus Christ!"

Tears gathered in Hannah's eyes. She wanted that relationship with all her heart! She fell to her knees beside the gravestone, the tears flowing down her cheeks unnoticed.

"Can I help you, little one?" a voice asked beside her.

Hannah looked up, straight into the concerned dark eyes of Alex DuVane. His face had lines she had not seen before, and his hair had silvered a little at the temples, but it was Master Alex! There was no doubt about it!

"Would you like me to pray with you?" he asked. "The sinner's prayer is very simple: Admit you are a sinner in need of salvation. Accept Jesus as your Savior. Ask Him to become Lord of your life. And thank Him . . ."

"Master Alex, don't you know me?" Hannah broke into his words.

He stopped and studied her in the dimming light. "Hannah?" he asked then. "Is it truly you, little one? I have wondered all these months what had become of you! Are your owners here? Did they bring you?" He looked around, as though to spot the Westons in the crowd.

"Master Alex," she said, taking hold of his hand and holding it as though she would never let go, "I have had a terrible life since I left you and Lettie in Charleston! I have worked very hard, and been beaten with a leather strap for my trouble. I have been forced to steal for my mistress. And now I am a runaway!"

"Oh, child, I am so sorry!" he said, putting an arm around her shoulders. "What can I do to undo the wrong I have caused you?"

"Nothing, Sir," she said. "Just don't make me go back!"

"Hannah, I would die first!" he exclaimed. "I had no idea those people would treat you that way! Had I suspected such, I would never have sold you to them. But how did you get here to this great revival?"

Hannah told him, as quickly as she could, how Mistress Weston had commanded her to steal for her once more, and how she had avoided the task by running away. She told him about the bloodhounds and about swimming the river. She told of Rufus and Jamaica and their children.

"Little one, of all the places you might have gone, it is a miracle that you ended up here, where you can be reunited with a friend! For I am your friend, Hannah. Please believe that!" he said.

"I believe that, Master Alex," she whispered.

"Best of all, little one, you can find God in this place, just as I found Him in the revival in Georgia a few months ago and gave Him my life. It is no accident that you are here, Hannah," he said fervently. "God has brought you to this place, at this time, so that He can become the best friend you've ever had."

Hannah leaned against his shoulder. "I want that, Master Alex," she said. "I want that relationship with my Maker that the preacher said I could get through the blood of Jesus."

When they had prayed, Hannah confessing her sins, asking for forgiveness, and accepting Jesus Christ as her Savior, he said, "Many of the preachers are not baptizing here, but I am baptizing a few people tomorrow afternoon, and I would consider it a great privilege to be the one to baptize you, little one."

Hannah nodded. "Whatever you say, Master Alex."

"What will you do after you leave here?" he asked then.

"I don't know, Master Alex. I just know I cannot go back to the tavern!"

"Of course, you cannot!" he agreed. "I would try to buy you back from them, but I have no money now. I have given all of it to the cause of Christ. I own a few items of clothing, my boots, some eating utensils, my horse, and a bedroll. And, of course, my Bible."

"It wouldn't do any good to try to buy me, anyway, Master Alex," she said, and she told him about Miss Rachel and her several attempts to buy her. "Mistress Weston would never sell me, especially now that I have run away. She enjoys punishing me too much."

"Hannah, Hannah!" he sighed. "What have I done to you? I am so sorry!"

"It's all right, Master Alex," she comforted him. Then she shared with him her thoughts about seeking work with Rufus and Jamaica.

"That might be a possibility, little one," he admitted. "I can't think of a better solution at the moment. But if their employer won't hire you, what then?"

"I don't know," she answered. Then she grinned up at him. "I'm a pretty good lady's maid."

"That you are, little one," he agreed. "And I can give you good references. However, we must not take lightly the fact that you are a runaway. If the Westons pursue it, you could be put to death!"

"I know," she said, suddenly wondering what had become of Bo. One thing was sure, the Westons had not caught him, at least not up until the time she had left the tavern.

"Well, come with me for now, and we will find some supper," he broke into her thoughts. "Then perhaps we can find your friends with the wagon and mules and ask about your chances of employment with their former master."

Once they had eaten, they began the search for her new friends, Master Alex leading her methodically from camp to camp, making inquiries.

Hannah followed, so caught up in a feeling of joy and peace that she felt her feet hardly touched the ground. She thought she knew exactly where she had left Rufus and Jamaica, but though they searched for two hours, they could not locate her friends.

"We obviously are not going to find them in this crowd, Hannah," Master Alex said finally. "However, you must have a place to stay tonight. As Jesus said, 'the foxes of the field have holes and the birds of the air have nests,' but Alex DuVane has no place to lay his head. I have been sleeping in the graveyard."

"I have been sleeping on the ground for several nights now, and I can sleep out there too," she assured him.

He shook his head. "Most of this crowd will camp out here tonight. But while many of them have been gloriously changed by their experiences here, some are the same rascals they were when they came, hanging around the crowd to see what mischief they can do. For your safety, little one," he urged, "seek refuge in the church tonight, up in the balcony. I will get you inside after they clear out the crowd. Tomorrow we will try again to find your friends."

"All right, Master Alex," she agreed. "I will do as you say."

True to her promise, Hannah climbed the ladder to the balcony of the church, spread her shawl on a backless wooden bench, and lay down. It was too hot to sleep, though, and she longed to go back to the graveyard, but she had promised Master Alex. Finally, she fell asleep, leaning her head on the windowsill to catch any air that might be stirring.

Early the next morning, when she backed down the ladder from the loft, Master Alex was waiting for her. He handed her a tin mug of milk and two biscuits with thick bacon between them.

After breakfast, she left him studying his Bible and went in search of Rufus and Jamaica. She thought she recognized the oak tree, but there were no mules, no wagon, and no familiar faces to greet her.

They must have gone home, she thought, *and there's no way I can catch up with them now.* They had talked about their former owner, but they had not mentioned where his land holdings lay. They could be anywhere in Kentucky!

What am I going to do now? she wondered. *How will I ever find a position, even with Master Alex's references?* She had no idea where to start. But her newfound peace was so deep that worry just slid right off of her, and she wandered contentedly among the campsites, where preachers mounted on stumps or wagons continued to exhort groups of listeners to repent and be saved.

That afternoon Master Alex baptized two men, three women, and Hannah in a quiet pool of a nearby creek. But the stillness of the water worried her, for the Gullahs believed that there must be an outgoing tide to carry away the sins.

As she came up out of the water, Hannah whispered to Master Alex, "Will this still water carry our sins away?"

"This water is not as still as it seems, for it moves gradually downstream under the rocks," he explained, "but it is not the water that takes away our sins, little one. The water is merely a symbol of the blood of Jesus."

After the baptism, Hannah claimed a spot in the graveyard where she could hear the service from the church. The preacher was not such a spellbinding speaker as the one from the night before, though, and she found her mind wandering until he said, "'There is neither Jew nor Greek, slave nor free, male nor female, for,' it says in Galatians 3:28, 'ye are all one in Christ Jesus.'"

Neither slave nor free, male nor female? Hannah thought. But she was still a girl, and if she were back in Frankfort, she would still be a slave. What did that verse mean?

"You slave owners must treat your former slaves as brothers and sisters in the Lord, as Paul admonished the slave owner, Philemon, when he sent back his runaway slave, Onesimus," the speaker continued. "And you former slaves are free in Christ!"

Hannah shifted her position against the gravestone. She had never heard the story of Philemon and Onesimus, not at the Praise House and not in her studies with Mistress Annabelle. Of course, Miss Rachel's Old Testament had no Galatians in it.

After the services, Master Alex sought her out to have supper with him, and she plied him with questions about the runaway slave, Onesimus. Master Alex opened his Bible, and they read the story together.

"Paul really was hinting for Philemon to set Onesimus free," he explained. "He is saying here that we all are equal in the sight of God."

That reminded Hannah of Miss Rachel's quotes from the Declaration of Independence: "All men are created equal . . . endowed by their Creator with certain . . . ." What kind of rights was it? *Oh, well,* she thought, *it doesn't matter what they call them. It's the rights that are important.* And Paul had said in Galatians 3 that there was neither slave nor free when a person had accepted Jesus Christ as Savior, as she had done last night. Still, one thing troubled her.

"But Paul sent Onesimus back to his owner, Master Alex," she insisted. "Does God expect me to go back to the Westons?"

"Paul sent Onesimus back with a plea that Philemon, a Christian brother, would treat his former slave as a brother in the Lord. But the Westons are not Christian brothers, little one. God would not want you to deliberately put yourself in such danger."

Hannah sighed. "Master Alex," she began.

"Don't call me master anymore, Hannah," he said. "I have always felt that slavery was an odious institution, and I look on you now as my daughter in the Lord."

"Yes, Master Alex," she began, then stopped. "What am I to call you?" she asked.

"Call me Alex."

"Oh, sir, I couldn't!" she protested.

"Then call me Mister Alex," he said, obviously relieved to find a title they both could accept.

"All right, Master . . . uh, Mister Alex. But what am I to do? If the Westons ever find me, they will take me back. After all, I belong to them."

"I know, little one. We must go back, I suppose, but only to get the Westons to sell you to your kind Miss Rachel. Then you will be free of them forever."

"Mistress Weston will never sell me, Mister Alex. Never! She would kill me first!"

"As long as you are a runaway you will never be truly free, for you know the punishment for runaway slaves is sometimes death, little one," he reminded her, his sad, dark eyes studying hers. "We must force Mrs. Weston to sell you." He was lost in thought for a few moments, then suddenly asked, "Hannah, have you ever seen Mrs. Weston steal anything—anything that could be identified?"

She shook her head. "I've not seen her take anything. She always made me do it." She stood thinking, trying to recall some incriminating incident. "I did hear Master Weston say once that she had caused them to flee from Georgia with the law on their heels."

"That's it!" he exclaimed, his frown replaced by a grin that set his dark eyes to dancing. "I think I can bluff our way through this, little one," he assured her, reaching out to tousle her curls. "You will belong to Miss Rachel by tomorrow night!"

Mistress Weston will never sell me, she thought, but she said nothing, and the next day Hannah rode back to the Brass Lion behind Alex DuVane on his horse.

Chapter Fifteen

The first time Hannah had ever seen Mistress Weston totally speechless was when she and Mister Alex walked into the Brass Lion just before dark the next evening.

"I'm sorry I ran away, mistress," Hannah began breathlessly. "Well, truthfully, I'm not sorry I went to the Great Revival and learned about Jesus, the Savior. Oh, it was wonderful, mistress! I wish you could have been there! But you can have Jesus as your Savior, too. It's so easy! All you have to do is confess . . ."

The mistress was staring at her like she had lost her mind. "Do you dare to preach to me, girl?" she said through clenched teeth.

"Oh, no, mistress!" Hannah cried. "But please let me tell you about Jesus, and how He died for our sins! I have had such peace since that night at Cane Ridge Meeting House when I asked Jesus to be my Savior. I know He has forgiven me, even for stealing from . . ."

"Shut up, you stupid girl!" the mistress hissed, throwing a glance at Alex DuVane.

Hannah swallowed the words she had been about to say. "Anyway, I'm sorry for all the trouble I caused you by running away," she said instead.

"It's all water under the bridge now, dear," Mistress Weston purred, with a sideways glance at Alex DuVane. "We will just put it behind us, and get on with running our tavern."

Hannah looked up in astonishment at the idea that the mistress would accept her back without question, without punishment! But Mistress Weston was smiling that thin, false smile that never quite reached her eyes.

Master Weston entered the public room from the back, and stopped when he saw Hannah. "I never thought I'd see the likes of you again, young'un!" he exclaimed. "Tired of wandering, are you? With nothing to eat and no place to sleep? Well, welcome home!" he said with a twisted grin. He went to the bar, picked up his jug, and sat down at the table.

"I have not brought Hannah back here to stay," Alex DuVane said. "I would never leave her here with you again!"

"But she is our slave, sir!" Mrs. Weston protested. "You sold her to us yourself!"

"And I am here to see that she is sold again, to the lady next door who has tried to buy her several times already."

"Never!" Mrs. Weston said. She turned to Hannah. "You will never see that woman again, girl! I know she . . ." She let her words die as Miss Rachel came through the back door.

"Hannah, is it really you?" she exclaimed. "I was coming back to the house from Miriam's grave, when I saw the two of you dismount and go into the tavern."

Hannah ran to Miss Rachel and was enveloped in a hug. "I'm so glad to see you, Miss Rachel," she whispered past the tears in her throat.

"But child, why have you come back here?" Miss Rachel asked. "I have missed you terribly and been concerned for your welfare, but when I heard you had run away, I was glad to know you weren't over here being beaten."

"Madame, I am Alex DuVane, a friend of Hannah's, and I have brought her back to see that she is sold to you, if you still want her," Hannah heard Mister Alex say behind her.

"Of course I want her!" Miss Rachel exclaimed. "I have tried to buy her several times, but Mrs. Weston . . ."

"The girl is my property, and she is not for sale," Mrs. Weston interrupted. "Especially not to you, Mrs. Crenshaw. I know you helped her plan her escape!"

"Oh, Mistress Weston, that's not true!" Hannah gasped. "Miss Rachel knew nothing about it. I had no plans. It was just that I could not steal for you again, and I knew I was in for another terrible beating if I refused. I just couldn't take it anymore."

"Mrs. Weston, I never would have sold Hannah to you had I suspected you would treat her so cruelly," Mister Alex said. "I insist that you sell her now to Mrs. Crenshaw."

"And I tell you, I will not!" Mrs. Weston declared. She folded her arms across her chest, and spread her feet, as though prepared to do battle right there.

Hannah glanced at Mister Alex and saw that he looked every bit as determined as Mistress Weston. "Then am I to assume you are ready to talk to the authorities concerning a certain matter still hanging over you in Georgia, Madame?" he asked.

Hannah saw doubt waver in the small, blue eyes. Then the woman's mouth curled into a sneer. "What do you know about Georgia? I have nothing hanging over me there!"

"Are you sure, Madame?" Mister Alex asked quietly, his fiery dark eyes holding hers.

Hannah saw doubt waver in Mistress Weston's eyes again. Then she tossed her head defiantly. "You have no proof of anything!"

"No, Madame, I do not," Mister Alex answered honestly. "But there are those who do. I assume you do not mind my letting them know where you are."

"Weston!" Mistress Weston's voice rose to a whine, but her husband busied himself with refilling his mug and ignored her.

"Think, Madame!" Mister Alex said. "Is it worth the risk just to keep one small slave girl? Sell Hannah to Mrs. Crenshaw, and I will not trouble you again."

"Name your price!" Miss Rachel urged.

A crafty look came to Mistress Weston's face. "One thousand dollars!" she crowed.

Hannah's heart sank. Mistress Weston had won, for she had named a price Miss Rachel surely would not pay. Not even her strong, husky brothers had brought so much!

"You will have your money as soon as the bank opens in the morning," Miss Rachel promised. "I will expect her signed papers at that time." She turned to Hannah. "Get your things, child."

"But you've given me no money for her yet!" Mistress Weston protested. "You can't just . . ."

"We can, and we will," Mister Alex said firmly, stepping protectively in front of Miss Rachel and Hannah. "You will get your money in the morning."

Hannah mentally inventoried her "things," and realized that all she owned was the faded yellow dress she wore. Her shoes had come apart. Her blue dress and her night shift had long since become rags. She had lost her last gold piece somewhere between Frankfort and Cane Ridge, and she certainly did not want Mistress Weston's old shawl!

"I'm ready, Miss Rachel," she said.

Miss Rachel raised her eyebrows, then she smiled and her dark eyes twinkled. She held out her hand. "Come along, child," she said. "You have two new dresses at my house, and anything else you need. For now, I think it's about time for a very late tea party. Won't you join us, Mr. DuVane?" She placed her right hand on his arm and reached for Hannah's hand with her left.

"Now, see here . . ." Mistress Weston began, but whatever she had planned to say was lost as two well-dressed men came through the front door.

"Can we get some supper here and a room for the night?" one of them asked.

Mistress Weston threw one last baleful glance at the three of them, then turned with a smile to her customers.

The men look prosperous, Hannah thought. *Will Mistress Weston do her own stealing tonight, as she must have done in Georgia? Well, at least it won't be me doing her thieving tonight!* she thought with relief as she, Miss Rachel, and Mister Alex crossed the yard to the tall brick house next door.

After they had finished a very pleasant tea, Miss Rachel showed Mister Alex to a room on the second floor overlooking the street. Then she led Hannah down the hall to a small yellow and white room overlooking the gardens at the back of the house.

Hannah knew the room well. She had cleaned it herself when she had worked for Miss Rachel. It had belonged to little Miriam. The little girl's rag doll with the beautiful painted china face still sat among the cushions on the window seat beneath the back window.

"This will be your room, Hannah," Miss Rachel said, walking briskly to the tall bed and turning back the covers. She took a nightshift from a dresser drawer and laid it across the foot of the bed. "That's one of mine and may be a little too long for you, but we will alter it to fit later. Now, climb into bed, dear, and I will see you in the morning."

"But Miss Rachel," Hannah protested, "this was Miriam's room!"

"I am well aware of whose room it was, Hannah," Miss Rachel said firmly. "And it's been empty too long. Good night, child." With that, she left the room, and Hannah heard her footsteps descending the stairs to her own bedroom on the first floor.

Hannah slipped out of her yellow dress and into Miss Rachel's nightshift. Holding it up out of the way, she climbed into the deep featherbed, pulled a light cover over her, and lay back against the soft pillows.

She could hardly believe she would be living here with kind Miss Rachel, using this lovely room, being treated like a child of the house! What good times she and Miss Rachel would have, working together, having tea, reading the Bible, putting flowers on Miriam's grave. And she would tell Miss Rachel about Jesus, the Messiah, whom she believed had not yet come, she thought drowsily as she fell into a deep sleep.

* * *

Suddenly, a shot rang out, followed by a piercing scream. Hannah awoke with a start. How long had she been asleep? There was shouting and running footsteps next door. Hannah jumped out of bed, threw off her nightshift, pulled on her dress, and ran down the stairs. As she raced out the door, she heard Mister Alex and Miss Rachel behind her.

They met Master Weston at the foot of the tavern stairs. "They've shot her!" he yelled. "They've shot Peg! I'm going after the doctor!"

"Is she dead?" Hannah called after him, but he was out the front door and gone.

Hannah climbed the stairs and saw Mistress Weston sitting on the floor of the hallway, leaning against the frame of the door to the big bedroom. She was holding a blood-soaked towel to her shoulder. The men, dressed in nothing but their breeches, were standing guard over her, one of them holding a gun.

"He shot me!" she cried to Hannah.

"And well I should have!" the man said. "I caught her with her hand under my pillow replacing my purse after she had lightened it a good bit!"

Mistress Weston had been caught in the act. Hannah was glad *she* had not been the one stealing for her this night!

Miss Rachel and Mister Alex reached the upstairs hall, and stood staring at the scene before them, both of them apparently speechless.

"Can I help you, mistress?" Hannah asked, not knowing what else to do or say. "Are you in pain?"

"Of course I'm in pain, you stupid girl!" she screamed. "I've been shot!"

"She'll live," the man without the gun said, slipping on his shirt and tucking it into his breeches.

Hannah heard the door open below them and footsteps climb the stairs. Then Master Weston appeared, followed by a man carrying a small black bag.

Once the doctor had treated and bandaged the gunshot wound in Mistress Weston's shoulder, each of the lodgers took her by an arm.

"We'll see how many purses she finds under the pillows at the jail!" one of them muttered as they hustled her down the stairs.

"I guess I ought to go bail her out," Master Weston said uncertainly. Then he straightened his shoulders. "But maybe a night or two in jail will put the fear of God into her about this stealing business."

"Will she be all right?" Hannah asked, wondering why she was concerned. The mistress certainly had never been concerned about her!

The master laughed. "Peg Weston is a tough old bird, young'un! It's the rest of them in that jail that had better look out!"

"Come, child," Miss Rachel said, "let's go home."

Hannah's heart leapt with joy, as memory came flooding back. She no longer had to say "Master Weston" or "Mistress Weston." She belonged to Miss Rachel now.

"I believe I will head on back to Cane Ridge," Mister Alex said when they were outside again. "The moon is bright, and I like traveling at night when the air is cooler."

He bent to give Hannah a hug. "I will be back to see you, little one," he promised. Then he turned to Miss Rachel, took her hand in his, and raised it to his lips. "Take good care of her, Mrs. Crenshaw," he said.

"Like my own child," Miss Rachel promised. "I plan to have manumission papers drawn up immediately so she will be free when she comes of age, or at my death."

Mister Alex smiled, gave them a half salute, and disappeared around the corner of the tavern. In a moment, Hannah heard his horse canter away down the dirt street.

Miss Rachel reached for her hand and led her toward the brick house. As they pushed through the boxwood hedge,

Hannah remembered that she would never have to pass through that hedge going toward the tavern again, and the horse-sweat odor was the sweetest scent she had ever smelled.